IDI'S ARK

and other stories

Robin Wrigley

Published by R M Wrigley, Verwood, Dorset

Survey Crew, Algeria, c.1973

Some of the stories in this collection have appeared online at
cafelitmagazine.uk

The following have been published in

The Best of CaféLit: Dinner for One, Do Pigeons ever get Bored? The
Bangkok Bash, A Bridge over Troubled Waters, Father van der Bosch's
Last Christmas, A Lost Lover

A Million Ways: No Direction Home
This Little World: Dorset Blue Vinney

Acknowledgements

First and foremost, I would like to extend my thanks to Roger & Penny Dale who initially inspired me to put this collection of stories into a book. They did all the hard work in editing my writing into some semblance of order.

Secondly, my partner, Anna Smith who has patiently listened to many of these stories over the years, as well as many other stories and anecdotes time and time again.

Thirdly, Pauline Howard for her technical advice and for organising the book's availability on Kindle.

Lastly, but certainly not least, Sarah Steele and the various members, present and past, of her Wimborne Writing Group who basically showed me by example how to construct a readable short story.

The Anthology

This collection of stories is the product of a man who, thanks to his occupation and thus his work in many different countries and cultures, has been able to distil a fraction of what he has experienced into story form.

The world is full of interesting people and I have been fortunate to have met probably more than my fair share. There are three major periods that have influenced my life: three years at boarding school, six years in the British Army and several decades as an expatriate.

Holiday in Mogadishu, Masta Mak, Mayday – the Mayaguez Incident, The Tallest Girl on the English Stage and *The Flying Bedstead* are to all intents and purposes real events that took place, as remembered by me. Any inaccuracy is unintentional.

I have in mind an old saying from Laos, (the closest I've been is Nong Khai across the Mekong River). *If you hear something, you must listen. If you see something, you can judge.*

Robin Wrigley
Verwood, Dorset, 2021

Idi's Ark
and other stories

Idi's Ark

The only one who knew the true events of the disappearance of the captain of the Kasanje Road ferry on Lake Victoria was a deaf and dumb fisherman called Dixon Brown. He had ferried him across the channel the night before the fact that both the captain and the month's takings went missing became public knowledge. But then nobody asked him.

Four weeks earlier, standing in the small, cluttered bridge of the *Good Luck Ferry*, the captain, Idi Kwangi, watched the usual mixture of vehicles and foot passengers boarding. He was more irritable than usual this morning. It was the first week of Ramadan and he would have given his right arm for a cigarette, were it not forbidden during daylight hours. He wasn't religious but found it added to his superiority as captain to abstain, also because he couldn't put up with the looks and comments if he openly broke the fast by smoking. Besides, many of the passengers knew him personally.

The level of his irritability hit a new high when he noticed a dilapidated Land Rover stalled across the gangplanks in its attempt to board the ferry. He reached for the microphone hooked on the shelf under the front windscreen, then he remembered it only worked at safety inspections.

Instead, he stuck his head outside the bridge door and yelled through cupped hands - the loud hailer was stolen two weeks previously along with two lifejackets - to the crew members lounging on some bales of rags, to get off their arses and push the offending vehicle either on or off the boat.

The crew looked back at Idi for a moment, surprised that they were actually being asked to do something. Seeing his brawny outstretched arm swinging wildly in a threatening manner, one by one they got up and moved towards the stricken Land Rover. They chose the path of least resistance and pushed it backwards off the gangplanks.

Two hours later and four hours behind schedule, the ferry set sail for the morning crossing to the Nakiwongo Road connection at Banga Beach. As they chugged across the channel, Godwin Nwange, a Nigerian Christian Pastor at Maranatha Lutheran church close to Idi's compound, entered the cabin and shook Idi's hand warmly.

'How's de old Ramadan going Idi?' Godwin's face broke out into a broad grin emphasised by the whiteness of his teeth.
'Oh, it ain't so bad you know.' There was no way he was going to let this guy know that he was in fact dying for a cigarette. The only reason he associated with Godwin was because he was his main source of distilled palm wine.

'Well I's take my hat off to you Idi. I just don't know how you do it and I don't even smoke.' Again Godwin broke out into a huge grin in sympathy for the big man, although it was interpreted as that of an oppressor mocking the afflicted.

'You hear about all dem Syrians and refugees drowning up north there? I mean how stupid can they be to get in dem boats without a proper captain? Maybe you should get a job up there Idi. You'd get 'em across wouldn't you? You'd be a local hero.'

'Only a dopey Nigerian like you would come up with something like that Godwin,' Idi replied with renewed irritability. But the seed was sown.

Several weeks later, following the Eid celebrations, the captain of the *Good Luck Ferry* disappeared. It was the talk of Lulongo town for weeks, mainly because the ferry never sailed that day. The owner was in Mecca attending the Hajj and nobody else knew how to find a replacement captain.
It was speculated that he might have fallen overboard while carrying out inspections on the vessel. There was talk of dragging the shoreline, but it was dismissed in favour of keeping a lookout every time they sailed with the new captain when the ferry resumed service, three days later.

A taxi driver at Nakiwongo Road, asleep in his car in order to be first in line the next day, was pleasantly surprised to get a fare into

Entebbe transporting this big guy in a smart sky-blue suit and sunglasses. For his life he couldn't understand why people wore sunglasses at night; he decided he must be a rapper or whatever they call them.

Idi's flight to Tripoli was something he would never forget. First a passport: Godwin's curate Gideon, a master forger, provided this complete with a near perfect Libyan visa. All for the promise of free ferry rides for life.

He had spent many an hour as a child watching planes passing overhead from Entebbe airport across the lake, but he had never given a thought as to how complicated it would be getting on one. But with the help of a very pretty air hostess who showed him the intricacies of fastening a seat belt, he soon got the hang of things. Relaxing back in his seat he smiled to himself thinking 'I could get used to this'.

Normally, if such a word ever applied in the Libyan capital, the arrival of a six foot four inch Ugandan with forged papers rambling on about being a volunteer sea captain would have resulted in immediate deportation, if he was lucky.

However, it transpired Idi was more than just lucky because he was passed from immigration control to a security agent; his saving grace had been his religion and occupation. There seemed no end to his good fortune. By pure chance the agent was a close friend and distant relation to the head of the western half of the country. He was aware they were looking into setting up a people-smuggling operation to rival the gross inefficiency of the system operating in Benghazi.

Idi, who spoke virtually no Arabic beyond some of the very basic words required in prayers, spent his time straining his ears and brain in vain attempts to understand what was being said about him. He had the look of a large performing bear that was being instructed in new tricks but was unsure how to make the first move as he glanced from one to the other. It was a worrying two days until finally, he was taken to what he felt must be a very important man's office. At last, he began to feel they were taking him seriously.

Ahmed Sergezi sat behind a splendid oak desk. It was completely bare, except for a crystal ashtray and a small glass cup of coffee on a gold saucer. He was of small stature, clean-shaven and dressed in an immaculate white shirt with a grandad collar under an expensive, well cut, grey silk two-piece suit.

Idi, on the other hand, stood like a schoolboy in front of a headmaster, fumbling the small bag he had been allowed to keep, his best suit now crumpled, after being worn continuously for nearly a week. He felt cheap and shabby in comparison to his host's immaculate attire. He had never felt so nervous in all his life, not since that day he made his maiden, solo voyage across Lake Victoria.

Ahmed was the first to speak. 'Do you speak English?' He spoke slowly, selecting his words carefully, and his enunciation was faultless and devoid of any accent.

'Oh yessir, I speak English as well as Lugandin and Swahili, sir.' Idi was so relieved to be spoken to properly in English.

'Good, take a seat. Would you like a drink of something, tea, coffee?'

'Thank you sir, just a glass of water would be nice.'

Ahmed made a slight movement with his right hand under his desk, and instantly Idi's escort stepped into the room. Ahmed spoke quietly in Arabic without looking at the man, and he left and returned with a large bottle of water and a glass on a silver tray and placed it in front of Idi.

The meeting was brief, probably no more than fifteen minutes. Having ascertained that Idi was a competent ship's captain and waving away his attempts to show his papers, it was explained to him what his job would entail. Ahmed wanted to give some genuine humane assistance to the hundreds of refugees passing through Libya en route to Europe. He would be assigned a vessel and then make his first voyage. The plan would be to sail from the main Tripoli docks north to the port of Marseilles, France. The authorities there will be expecting the ship to pick up a new cargo of wheat. For this service he would be paid five thousand US dollars per month. Later, in his accommodation, he would be instructed in detail what the plan entailed.

Ahmed's parting words were imparted in a stern and serious manner. 'This is the start of a very important operation. Our cousins in Benghazi have been acting very stupidly, wasting our migrants to crowded ports and in some cases losing them completely to the bottom of the sea. Our plan is to distribute people to major ports on the western side of the Mediterranean. We won't waste time with any of the islands like Malta. In future we may even deliver to other countries via the Gibraltar Straits. You will go down in history as the first captain delivering the forefathers of what will become the new Islamic Europe. Understood? You may go now.' With that he summoned the minder again.

'Thank you, sir, thank you. You can count on me sir.' The first captain! Five thousand dollars a month; Idi's head was spinning but Ahmed paid him no attention and was speaking furtively into a mobile phone. The minder ushered Idi out of the office.
He was driven to a small single storey house surrounded by a high wall. As they drew up outside the gates an armed guard in army uniform swiftly unlocked it, allowing the car inside before closing the gates behind them. Idi assumed they were close to the sea as he could smell the salt in the air. Inside he was shown a bedroom complete with a bathroom attached. On the bed was a complete change of clothes including a set of navy blue coveralls and safety boots. He was then ushered into a small dining room where a meal was laid out. On the wall a television was showing an Arabic programme about farming.

Later, having showered and changed into his first clean underwear for a week, he lay down on the bed and tried to take it all in, but was asleep within minutes, dreaming a thousand dreams.

He awoke early and showered again before putting on his new uniform complete with a matching navy blue baseball cap emblazoned with oak leaves and the title 'Captain'. He looked at himself in the wall mirror, pleased that everything fitted him perfectly.

In the dining room a selection of fresh fruit, yoghurt and pastries had been left on the table complete with a vacuum flask of hot water, tea, coffee and sugar sachets.

As he finished eating and was on his second cup of coffee, the side door opened and his minder from the day before reappeared.

'You finished?' His question was short and terse. He didn't wait for an answer but moved to another door and held it open indicating Idi to enter.

Inside this room, the spacious rectangle had been laid out in conference room fashion. The opposite wall was plastered with various maps and hydrographic charts. The end wall held a whiteboard with a pull-down screen rolled up above it. The most noticeable feature of the room, considering its size, was the total absence of any windows.

Seated at a long conference table were two young, bearded men in black turtle-neck sweaters, black jeans and sandals. They did not introduce themselves and Idi was silently motioned to take a seat opposite them.

'Listen and do not interrupt; you can ask questions at the end,' his minder said quietly with a hint of menace. The following two hours left Idi wondering just what he had let himself in for. The two young men took turns in describing his intended voyage. It would take place in two days' time. He would be in charge of a 5,000 ton cargo ship called the *Star of the Sea* and registered in Monrovia. He would be accompanied by a Libyan crew of ten, who would be armed at all times. Their leader would be a lady called Amira. She would act as second in command and would in reality be in charge of the vessel and could countermand any of his decisions at any time. All radio contact with Tripoli would be kept to a minimum and would be in Arabic.

During pauses amongst the information being relayed by first one and then the other of the two speakers, Idi (forgetting his initial instructions not to interrupt) tried in vain to ask questions but was silenced each time.

The last item was the matter of his outgoing cargo. On board and ready to sail would be 1500 Arab passengers of various nationalities.

They would travel in the hold for the first half of the journey. All hatches would be left open to ensure they had sufficient fresh air. They would have been given sufficient food and water to last the duration.

The final part of the plan would take place under darkness when as many as possible of the women and children would be allowed on deck and would remain there until they reached French territorial waters. He would explain to the French or any other authorities that he had saved all these people from a flotilla that was in danger of sinking. All of the passengers had been well briefed on their cover story. At least one member of each family had undergone a month's intensive French language tuition to assist their integration.

By now Idi had so many questions that he couldn't think of where to start and so simply said, 'I think I've got all that sirs. Do you think I could have notebook and pen to make some notes please?'

'There will be no need and no taking notes. You sail at dawn the day after tomorrow. If you do well you will be richly rewarded, as our leader is a generous man. But if you fail you will wish you had not been born. Tonight, you will see your ship at five o'clock. Be ready.' With that he was ushered out of the room.

Back in his bedroom Idi stretched out on the bed with his hands behind his head. That last remark was a little unsettling, but he could do it. A broad grin spread across his face. 'Godwin was wrong. I won't just be a hero. I'll be an international hero.' He rolled onto his side and waited patiently for five o'clock to come around.

The Tallest Girl on the English Stage?

Christmas week at school was always the most exciting - especially the thought of being home with our families, but also the knowledge that we were halfway through the period of short days and dark mornings.

In that week was also the excitement of the annual cross-country run which every boy with two legs was obliged to enter, and on the last night of term there was the Christmas pantomime. For me the run was simply something one endured. Not being particularly good at distance running and being the kind of boy who felt that if I couldn't win there was little point exhausting oneself, when having fun mucking around with the tailenders was available.

The panto was a different thing altogether, and I, and several other boys coached by Mr Mays, one of the three housemasters, spent many a long evening learning lines and painting the flats for the show. Mrs Clarke the matron also helped in the advice and the sewing of various costumes and makeup.

Mr Mays always provided the script and then everyone in the Drama Group spent time editing it to be topical for our school, in particular lines which would poke fun at various teachers and staff. These lines would always bring the house down; our headmaster Mr G.A.F. Clarke naturally nicknamed Gaffer, and no relation to matron, came in for considerable mickey-taking, as did the youngest housemaster Mr Basil Smith, known as Bart.

That last afternoon was a complete buzz of activity. Getting the scenery in place, swotting lines and eventually makeup and then dressing into our costumes. Charlie Woollard and I were the ugly sisters.

First on stage was Ronald Blick, cast as the Fairy Godmother, who acted as narrator in between scenes. Poor lad, when the whole show was over he discovered the lipstick kindly donated by matron was the 'kiss-proof' type which no amount of rubbing would remove. The next day he was forced to travel home with these lovely bright red lips and take enormous amounts of ribbing that morning at breakfast, particularly from the first years.

The opening scene was designed to set the mood of the audience and ensure that everyone was in for an evening of belly laughs. It did not fail. It was a beach scene and Charlie and I would enter from stage left wearing bikinis. The pair of us were pretty skinny and being dressed in fairly skimpy bikinis did much to emphasise this. No doubt we looked more like entertainers in a prisoner of war camp than a school panto. The audience were delighted and the laughter and applause almost shattered the windows. I think we both found it quite difficult not to react to our reception and keep a straight face.

But the next couple of steps we made really brought the house down and very nearly stopped the entire show. Charlie accidentally stepped on a drawing pin. The pain sent him howling and clutching his foot, nearly knocking over the nearest scenery flat.

The house loved it, mistakenly thinking it was all part of the show. But just like true professionals we quickly recovered. The offending tack was removed from Charlie's heel, a quick wipe with a hankie, and we were back on to the script and the audience were totally ignorant of the mishap.

It was my part in that last pantomime before I left school that caused the Deputy Head to write in my final report later that summer 'The tallest girl on the English stage?' He followed it up by dubbing me 'A charming flâneur' which sent me rushing to the library and a dictionary. Mr Boyd-Roberts knew a thing or two.

Canned

The flight to Cannes from London was thankfully short in comparison to the previous leg from Houston. Marvin leaned forward to catch sight of the land below, past Dolores who had the advantage of the window seat. She had clutched his hand as she always did once landing was imminent. Landings and take-offs, the only times that his wife ever sought to hold his hand.

This was their first time back in Europe in over forty years, when Marvin had been a fighter pilot based in England in the sixties. For him it was a time of fond memories, but not for Dolores. She had not enjoyed life in England. For her the only place she felt happy was in Brazos County, Texas. For this reason he never fully understood why his wife had suggested returning to Europe for their wedding anniversary.

Though it was many years since he sat in the cockpit of a fighter jet, the training for sensing potential danger was always there. Once you left the ground those deep ingrained routines return. The rigorous training in the art of escape and evasion exercises in combat leaves an indelible mark in aircrew personnel.

The following day they walked into a smart restaurant fifteen minutes from the hotel, around eight o'clock in the evening. June the 15th, their forty-fifth wedding anniversary. Once they were seated and their drinks had been ordered and served she turned to him and said, 'I suppose you are wondering why the hell I chose England and France for our anniversary this year.'

Marvin took a sip from his martini, looked around the restaurant and then back at his wife, narrowing his eyes before saying, 'To be honest Dolores, it beat the shit out of me after all the moaning and groaning you did back when I was posted there. But as usual, whatever blows your dress up. As for Cannes, if I recall you didn't want to come here when the other wives arranged that trip.'

'And it never occurred to you why I didn't, did it?' she retorted, 'but I knew why you wanted me to go; just so you could carry on with that gal in the God-awful bar in Oxford! Didn't think I knew that did you?'

'So how come you didn't say anything?' He felt a need to respond although he was past caring.

'Because it would have caused a scandal, denials and worse; there was also a small matter of the kids and my wedding vows, you asshole.'

Marvin signalled the waitress for another drink, holding his glass up and tapping it with his forefinger. He turned back to Dolores. 'Did you get me all this way to tell me this? You really are something else Dolores – you know that? But then I just knew you were planning something like this, but I guess I misjudged you. I never thought you had the guts. So where do we go from here?'

'I know where I'm going. You have two weeks looking at the young gals in their bikinis, wishing you were fifty years younger. Me? I'm off to start a new life with someone who cares for me and wants to spend time with me. Something you haven't done in God knows how long.' With that she got up, looked at him with naked loathing and left the restaurant. It was the last time he ever saw her.

He casually looked around the restaurant in order to see if anyone had noticed the scene. But nobody appeared to have done so and frankly he didn't damn well care if they did. He contemplated what to do next; another dirty martini would help him decide, so he signalled the waitress and gave his order, but not before speaking briefly into his cell phone.

Two hours later, having finished his dinner, wine, coffee and two cognacs he paid his bill, left a generous tip along with a knowing smile for the waitress and left the restaurant and headed up the street without the vaguest notion of where he was going. Certainly not back to the hotel. The night was young and, God damn it, he was free to do whatever he chose. Dolores had made that crystal clear.

During the time since she had left Marvin at the restaurant, Dolores had been busy. Back at their hotel she went straight to their room and packed her carry-on bag with her jewellery and overnight essentials; she planned to leave the majority of her clothes along with Marvin as part of her complete separation from the unhappiness of her past life. She took her passport from the room safe, changed the SIM card on her cell phone, and made a brief call.

'It's done; I'll see you at the hotel in Paris as soon as you can get there. Have a safe flight.' With that she gathered her belongings and headed for the lift.

In the foyer she explained to the somewhat surprised receptionist that she had received some bad news from home – a death in the family – but her husband would still honour their reservation and would be along later.

'Would you like me to order you a taxi?'

'No thanks, I'll be fine,' and with that she made for the main door and down the steps into the street below. The hotel had been carefully selected to be within walking distance of the railroad station; she turned right and headed in the direction following the signs she had seen on arrival. She wanted to leave without a trace in case Marvin took it into his head to follow her in an attempt to change her mind. She felt quite confident of completing her plan, and it was unlikely that he would follow her, but it was better to be sure, as time was precious, to make her booking. There was a bounce in her step; she was excited in her new-found freedom and the thought of taking the sleeper to Paris. Marvin would never think of riding a train. Flying was all he ever cared for, besides golf, martinis and Mexican sluts.

At the corner of the block she stood looking up at the various direction signs when a youth, dressed in a bright red sweatshirt and white jeans suddenly appeared and said in clear accented English, 'Hi, can I help you? Are you looking for the station?'

His sudden appearance startled her initially as she hadn't noticed him until he spoke, and regaining her composure she replied, 'Yes, I am but it's okay thanks, I can see I need to turn up here.' She started to skirt around him.

'I must help you, it is not safe for you to walk through this area alone at night,' and before she could resist he had taken her trolley carry-on from her grasp and gestured graciously for her to walk alongside him away from the main street.

'Don't be afraid. It is not a problem to help you as the station is on my way home. I have just finished work and am on my way home to my mother.'

The mention of his mother had a calming effect and she fell into step alongside him.

'It really is very kind of you,' she turned and smiled at him. 'What kind of work do you do?' But she never heard the answer. A hand came from behind her and over her face and mouth, jerking her head violently to one side as she was manhandled into a small yard at the rear of the business premises, empty except for three rubbish carts.

Her guide had been joined by another youth; quickly and efficiently they stripped off her jewellery and stuffed it inside her handbag. At the same moment a battered white Peugeot pick-up pulled up and they threw her carry-on into the back. The newcomer lifted the lid of one of the industrial rubbish carts and the pair of them hoisted Dolores's unconscious body inside and slammed the lid shut. They scanned up and down the street to be sure they had not been seen; one of them snatched up her handbag and the pair jumped inside the pick-up and the vehicle took off at speed. The driver drove carefully checking for any sign of a potential hazard or the police. The whole episode had taken less than three minutes, not a word was spoken; it was executed in deadly, cold, rehearsed routine.

Back in the rubbish cart Dolores's inert body lay at an awkward angle. She appeared to be craning her neck over her right shoulder. The reason was her neck had been broken by the force her assailant had used when he snapped her head to one side. Her body had started to cool down, as a dark stain started to grow on the leg of her khaki cotton trousers; her right knee was pressed into a tray of used olive oil. A large rat crawled out from underneath her shoulder and started sniffing round her face, a face locked in a permanent look of sheer terror, eyes wide open, searching for the person she would never see.

Once in their apartment the leader of the group tapped his phone and said in English, 'It's done. Leave the rest of the money as agreed.'

At the Oddfellows Arms

Diary 3rd October 2015: WSG – 5 days – Oddfellows – 1900. DT12 2CX

Sitting in what the Poms call a greasy spoon next to what passes for a major road, somewhere north of Bath, I recapped on today's destination. I was booked to upgrade the IT system in a private (sorry, public) school in a small Dorset village called Wootton-St-Giles.

When I started my company, *OzTech – Will Travel*, three years ago, I had a wife called Trish. We came to the UK via the rest of the world, from Melbourne where I taught computer science at Melbourne University and Trish taught English at Hawthorne High. My only claim to fame in that period is that the WikiLeaks founder, Julian Assange, attended one of my lectures but left half-way through. Some people have said I look like him, but Trish says he's better looking. Maybe I should have seen the writing on the wall way back then.

The *Will Travel* part of my business card is what caused me my current single status. I made good money out of the fact that (a) I knew my way round educational IT systems having suffered their shortcomings as a lecturer and (b) I was prepared to work before eight o'clock in the morning and at weekends.

But my being on the road like this did not suit my marriage. Trish liked the benefits the money brought us. It allowed me to put down a deposit on a small unit in Isleworth where she did her best to teach Pommie kids to learn English up to the level of their Asian neighbours.

While I was chasing my arse all over the country, putting out fires in Britain's piss-poor educational IT systems, Trish found the attentions of Darren, the school's PE teacher, too hard to resist. So now Darren is bouncing up and down on my mattress while I currently suffer the dubious hospitality of Britain's finest B&Bs.

Tonight I am due to stay at the Oddfellows Arms in Wootton-St-Giles. It is one of the few places that I really enjoy visiting simply because there I had met this delightful old bloke called Lionel.

I first met Lionel in the Oddfellows two years ago. He was the sole customer that night besides me. The barmaid looked incapable of putting two words together, so I opted to introduce myself to him.

It was quite obvious that he was not used to people talking to him and I rather got the impression that my intrusion was not altogether welcome. I think it was my accent that saved me, that and another pint of the dreadful warm Badger Beer, before he opened up. Over several evenings he told me his life story. He was getting up there in years and apart from his hearing not being the best, he was mentally sharp as a needle.

He had run away from home at sixteen, home being a local farm where he worked for his father along with his two younger brothers. That was in the summer of 1937, shortly before the outbreak of the Second World War. He had made it to Southampton, worked a short time as a cleaner in a seamen's hostel, and wangled his way on as a deckhand on a Scandinavian barque – one of the tall ships transporting grain between England and Australia. It didn't take long, risking his life shinning up and down rigging, to realise he was not cut out for life at sea, so he jumped ship in Victoria and made his way to Queensland where he found work in the sugar-cane fields.

The work conditions were terrible, even though he was used to long hours on his father's place and not afraid of hard work, but the tropical heat, snakes, spiders and cane-toads were best summed up in his words that 'a day up there took a year off a man's life'. It was also accident riven; he showed me his left hand missing two fingers, the result of a miss-timed cut with a machete.

He chuckled about the abuse he suffered as an Englishman and how the locals never missed an opportunity to call him a Pommie Bastard. The First World War was still very raw in their memories and they took the actions of Winston Churchill's campaign in Gallipoli as being Lionel's personal responsibility. I was able to sympathise here as my own grandfather had suffered himself as a 'ten-pound tourist' back in the fifties when he first arrived as a migrant.

When the Second World War started he fronted up with his best mate to volunteer, but was instantly rejected because of the injury to his hand, so he went back to cutting sugarcane.

He wrote from time to time in an attempt to patch his relationship up with his family, but they never replied. Then, two years after the outbreak of war, he got a letter saying both his brothers had volunteered even though they were exempt. They had been posted to North Africa and both were killed; a direct hit on their position in Mersa Matruh. Reluctantly, he knew then he would need to go back and help his father run the farm.

There was no killing the fatted calf when Lionel arrived home. In the village some thought of him as a coward, while others reckoned he came back in order to inherit the farm. His father's attitude didn't help, but he took it all in silence; there was no point in trying to explain.

The first Armistice day after the war, he was walking home after a couple of pints in the Oddfellows when he was set upon by several men from the village. They beat him up pretty badly. That beating was the final straw. Overnight he became very bitter and used every opportunity to argue with anyone about the stupidity of war. It all added to his unpopularity; the most disastrous factor was that he never married.

His father never understood his actions and their relationship deteriorated further right up to his mother's death and got even worse once she was gone. The final blow came when his father died leaving his entire estate to his niece, his sister's daughter. His only saving grace was that his cousin, now legal owner, felt sorry for him and allowed him to continue living in the family home and running the farm until his retirement.

It was just after seven in the evening when I pulled into the car park behind the Oddfellows Arms. I walked into the bar and looked in the direction of the window seat where Lionel always sat. To my surprise and disappointment his chair by the window was empty. A middle-aged couple, whom I vaguely recognised, sat at a table near the fire and three young lads were propping up the bar. They stopped their conversation and turned to stare at me. The barmaid was a hard faced young girl with heavy makeup, a black tee shirt and brassy looking bangle ear rings. I had not seen her on previous visits.

'What can I get you?' She attempted to sound pleasant, but I heard only indifference; I wasn't a regular and therefore granted service not friendship. It was a reception that I was very familiar with but had not expected here. I hesitated: if Lionel wasn't here, I didn't particularly want to join this lot at the bar or drink on my own.

'Um, I was looking for Lionel, has he been and gone already?'

'Who?' She screwed up her face in a most unattractive way.

'He means Jezza, Debs. You know the old bloke who died last week,' the smallest of the three piped up with a nasty smile on his face. The other two sniggered; it was a private joke and I was not privy to it.

I ignored them and repeated my question to the barmaid. 'No, I mean Lionel the old fellow who comes in most nights and sits over there by the window.' I pointed to his usual position. 'Surely you must know him?'

'She ain't been 'ere long,' the same youth drawled, 'so she wouldn't know 'is name 'cos we always calls 'im Jezza 'cos he's like that bloke in the Labour party.'

'You mean Jeremy Corbyn: why do you think he's like him?'

'Yeah, that's 'im – 'cos they's both too scared to go to war.' His two friends almost collapsed with laughter and the barmaid also smiled as if she understood the joke.

I'm not sure whether I felt disappointed at the fact I wasn't going to see Lionel, or angry at the sheer rudeness of these three idiots. It was all I could do to stop myself from knocking the grin off of the face of this little shit. Instead I turned to the barmaid.

'Give me a pint of lager please, anyone will do, my palate can't distinguish one pint of Pommie piss from another.' I waited while she pulled it, took a sip and then said. 'Do you three know anything about Lionel at all, I mean really know?'

'Course we does – he buggered off to where I reckons you're from, and left his two brothers to join up and get killed. Back here he makes a bloody nuisance of himself every year when the old blokes come back for a pint after their parade in Blandford.'

'You are right up to a point. That being he did go to 'where I'm from' as you put it and while he was out there the war started and his two brothers were indeed killed.' Oh, I would so like to knock the sneer of this kid's face.

'See – what did I tell you, shit-scared he was just like that silly old bugger in the Labour party and that's why we calls 'im Jezza.' All three of them had stopped smiling now and had taken on a sinister threatening look about them. I realised I'd better be a little bit diplomatic here or I might be in for some trouble.

'Let me tell you a little story lads. When Lionel was a bit younger than you he was working on his dad's farm. This was a bit after the First World War. He didn't like working here because he wanted to have a life of his own. Money in his pocket, see life outside the village which in the 1930s must have been a lot different than it is today. He left home at the age of sixteen, two whole bloody years before the outbreak of the war. He did try and join up, in Australia, but was rejected because of his injured hand.'

'Good timing though, weren't it?' they were quietening down and beginning to listen.

'Yes, it was as it turned out, but how was he to know? He got himself to Southampton and signed on one of the big clippers transporting grain to Australia. You've seen those tall ships in books and movies. Can you imagine what it must have been like at sea in those days? All I can say is it doesn't sound like something a boy who is easily scared would do, does it?'

There was no answer now so I continued the tragic story that Lionel had told me over several evenings during my two previous visits. But I could tell they weren't interested so I cut the story short. I finished my drink, made a mental decision not to stay here tonight and was about to go. As I turned to go one of the other lads said, 'You're not that bloke from WikiLeaks, are you?'

'No,' I replied, 'he's my younger brother. You can tell us apart as he's much better looking than me.' I picked up my bag and headed out to the car park. It was handy for the school, but I'm buggered if I was staying here no matter how far the next place was.

The White Cadillac

Inspired by Kate Chopin's short story Désirée's Baby, 1893.

Eleanor finished her breakfast, rinsed the cup and bowl under the cold faucet and went outside. Around the back of her small wooden house she pulled the cotton cover off the Cadillac. Having folded the sheet as best she could, she stowed it under the back of the house and stood admiring the car.

It had been given to her by the old judge in town when he retired. She had cleaned both his house and his office on Main Street for twenty-three years, never missing a single day. It was her retirement present from his employ before he moved interstate. At the time she could not drive; she didn't even have a driving licence. Her brother had to collect it for her and then spend every spare moment showing her how to control the beast. She passed the test on the second attempt and for the first time, was able to drive the car home, all on her own. She felt like a queen even if there was no crowd to wave to.

Her biggest regret was that her house was isolated, sitting on the edge of a cotton field where their grandfather had built it, two generations back. It meant there was never anyone to witness her driving home in her own Cadillac. Alone in her own little world she still got a thrill out of standing back and admiring its solid shape once it was dusted down, the windows and mirrors polished.

Every Sunday morning she would either drive to church or simply go out for a drive for the thrill of doing so. She had no kin left after her brother died, no husband or children, so she was free to please herself. The white Cadillac was her companion. She went back inside to change.

In the small town of Horaceville, Eddie and Katya were coming up for their first anniversary living in the condominium that Eddie's parents had provided the deposit for as a wedding present. They had met at a basketball game in Houston. Katya had reluctantly agreed to accompany her brother to the Houston Rockets' game after his girlfriend stood him up.

At the end of the second quarter she had excused herself by saying she wanted to use the powder-room. She was bored as she never really understood why people could get so excited by two teams of giraffe-like men chasing each other from end to end of a wood-floored rectangle in an attempt drop a large orange ball through a hoop mounted on a board. Each time they managed it the crowd went wild. It all seemed so stupid and the three boys behind them were so loud.

Coming back from the restrooms and looking around for a refreshment outlet she literally bumped into Eddie who was carrying an armful of popcorn and beers. The bump caused beer to splash out of the plastic cups all over his trainers. He was angry at first until he realised how pretty she was as she put her hands to her face in pure shock at having caused the accident.

'Oh sorry, please I not see you.' Eddie wasn't sure which he found the most attractive – her appearance or the foreign accent. He was smitten.

'You don't worry one little bit. Just stay there while I give this to my friends, and I'll be right back.' He shot down the steps to his row spilling even more beer as he went, dumped the refreshments with his friend and rushed back to Katya, who against all the advice her brother had given about not talking to strangers, stood there waiting for the young man. Six months later they were married.

Eddie was so excited about Katya's pregnancy he got up early on Sunday morning in order to give his parents the news face to face. He knew they would be so excited at the thought of becoming grandparents, even though his mother had strongly advised him to delay having a family until they were better prepared. This was too good to be phoned or texted, their usual means of communication these days.

He decided to take Katya's Mazda sports car with the top down and eased it out of the driveway as quietly as possible so as not to wake her; he hoped she was still sound asleep. It was a bright October morning as he turned into East Parkway. If only the weather in East Texas was always like this Eddie thought to himself, instead of having to go to work encased in air-conditioning to avoid the usual heat and humidity.

Half a mile along the Parkway he came to a red light at the intersection with Juniper Drive. A white Cadillac Seville sat in the outside lane; the driver was an old black lady, patiently waiting. Eddie figured if he didn't get by her now, he would be following her for the next three blocks, so he pulled alongside her into the right turn lane. Being Sunday and quiet he could wait until the lights changed without blocking the lane for other cars.

He looked across at the old lady. He could only see her from the chin upwards as she was so small in the big sedan. She wore a bright green brimmed hat decorated with a large red rose on the right hand side. She must have sensed she was being observed and just looked straight ahead.

It amused Eddie. For the love of God he never understood why black folk always had to bedeck themselves with ridiculous hats. He went on to inspect the car. It was polished and appeared to be in good condition. Probably worth more than her house, he mused.

The light turned to green, and Eddie gunned the sports car into life and with a slight squeal of rubber was able to move into the main lane in front of the Cadillac. The old lady was just selecting 'drive', encouraged by the Chevrolet pick-up sitting behind her impatiently beeping.

Forty minutes later Eddie pulled into the driveway of his parents' house in Melody Oaks. His father was outside, bent picking up the Sunday newspaper. As Eddie climbed out of the car he was greeted with his Dad's usual sardonic attitude. 'What d'you want bothering respectable folk on a Sunday morning? I see you're still driving that rice burner. Don't tell me that cute gal you married seen the light of day and skedaddled back to Russia?

'It's always good to know I'm welcome home pop. No, Katya is fast asleep in bed and her car is a damn sight better than that gas guzzlin' monster you drive.' His reply had more warmth and genuine humour than that of his father. 'Where's mom?'

'Not sure, she might have run off to Mexico with the gardener, she's threatened to often enough. Then again she might be in the kitchen watching some crap on television.' He turned and started for the open garage door; Eddie followed behind. They never shook hands or hugged or anything, it was just the way his father was. It wasn't helped that this was his father's second marriage, and he was, in truth, old enough to be Eddie's grandfather.

Inside the house his father made off to his den armed with a cup of coffee and the newspaper. His mother was indeed in the kitchen nursing a large vacuum plastic tumbler of iced tea and glued to an old episode of Dallas she had found on an obscure satellite channel.

'Who were you talking to Wilbur?' she said to her husband's back as he disappeared through the interior door. Eddie grabbed her from behind and kissed the top of her head. She all but spilled the contents of her iced tea in her lap.

Eddie darling, how lovely to see you, what brings you here this morning? Not bad news I hope?' She swung the swivel chair round to face him and beamed with pleasure at seeing her only child.

'Far from it Mom, in fact I have some great news. You are going to be a grandmother, Katya's expecting!' He was so excited to get the news out he couldn't wait until his father was there.

The smile instantly dropped from her face, which caught Eddie unawares. He knew she had counselled him to wait a while, but he was sure she was going to be as thrilled as he was once the pregnancy was in progress. 'Have you told your father yet?' His mother got up from her chair and walked over to the door his father had just gone through and silently closed it.

'No, I didn't get the chance. What the hell's going on mom? You're really scaring me.'

'Sit down Eddie, this isn't going to be easy for me.' He did as he was bid and sat on one of the breakfast chairs.

'There is something I never ever told you, or your father for that matter. I am from a mixed-race family. My grandmammy was black.' The words hit him like a sledgehammer. In a flash all the racist words he had used in the past came flooding back; everything that had been said around the dinner table when he was growing up.

'So you're worried that our baby turns out black, a genetic throwback, is that it?' She merely nodded her head as she burst into tears.

He had heard enough. There was nothing more to say. He jumped up and ran outside, climbed into the Mazda and reversed out into the street as fast as he could. He heard the sound of a car's horn and looked right just in time to see the white Cadillac coming straight at him.

The little old lady in the green hat, her mouth wide open forming a scream and her eyes bulging, could do nothing to avoid him.

You stupid n…' but he never completed the word as the solid body of the Cadillac crashed into the driver's door of the flimsy sports car and drove him sideways, twenty feet along the road.

The Loneliness of a Mistress

Normally Helen only had one phone call on Saturday mornings; today it was a different caller. At eight-thirty, just as she was about to get into the shower, her sister-in-law called from Spalding.

Helen's brother James had died the previous night just before midnight. She took the news very calmly as though she was expecting it, when in actual fact she didn't even know he had been unwell. They had not spoken since her birthday back in April. It was now November. How had they drifted this far apart? It was as though Twickenham was the other side of the world from Spalding instead of just under a hundred and fifty miles, a little over three hours by car.

Instead of continuing on into the shower she poured herself a coffee from the percolator and sat down at the kitchen table. If there had been a cigarette handy, she would have lit up even though she hadn't smoked in twenty years and more. For a second she thought to search the place for one, but knew the search would be fruitless.

She looked at her reflection in the glass front of the kitchen cabinet. She often chose to look at herself this way. The glass cover was kinder than any mirror. James was dead; her brother was gone, never to be seen again. Guilt started to sweep over her. Why had she not made more attempts to see him and his family? Come to that, she consoled herself, why hadn't they kept in contact with her?

She got up and carried the coffee through into the lounge and flopped down onto the sofa. 'Oh Christ, Greg, why the hell aren't you here to share this with me?' she said to a photo of a middle-aged man on the wall opposite. But it was Saturday.

Helen, and Greg Weidner, her boss, had been lovers for just over thirty years. It had started on her twenty-fifth birthday when he offered to take her for dinner as compensation for keeping her late that evening. He was a vice-president of the Europe and Africa operations of an American independent oil company. He was fifteen years her senior and married. Thirty years; when she thought about it, and she often did, it still amazed her that it had ever started, let alone continued this long. He wasn't particularly attractive. About the only compliment she could ever think to pay him was that he was good at his job. He knew the business inside out, and he put in more hours than anyone else in the office. The other secretaries called him 'the man with no legs' because they rarely saw him the other side of his desk. He was sitting behind it when they arrived in the morning and still there when they went home.

As unfaithful as he was to his wife and family, Helen matched it with her faithfulness to him. She never told a soul, not even her mother, and certainly none of her co-workers, although she often wondered if any of them had twigged it. Sometimes, in the early days, she tested them with clever little subterfuges just to try and draw them out on the subject, but to no effect.

She had the advantage of being the vice-president's personal assistant and used the privileged position to keep her distance from the rest of the staff, particularly the younger men whom she judged would ask her out if she gave the slightest hint of a chance.

During her parents' lifetime her lack of boyfriends left them totally confused. One weekend when she had travelled up to Spalding to visit them, as her father had just suffered a heart attack that eventually led to his death weeks later, her mother questioned her closely. She admitted that they thought she might be gay and too afraid to tell them. She was quick to put her right and explained that she had dated several men but had simply not found the right one. She told her that she had developed into a career woman and was not interested in a husband and a family.

Her mother had died two years later of cancer. That only left James; now she was alone apart from her sister-in-law and two nieces. Their family name had gone with James' death. Her father never had any brothers. It wasn't something she had ever thought about before and wondered why she was doing so now.

She stood up and looked out of the lounge window at the backs of the houses around her flat and focused on a solitary pigeon on the fence. Often there were two, but she supposed it had also lost its mate. She started to weep silently. It had just occurred to her that it was remembrance Sunday tomorrow. She had never felt so alone in her life.

A Close Call

'Mr Bannister, tonight will be the most critical period for your daughter. If she can pull through the next twelve to twenty-four hours, she should have a good chance of a full recovery.' The girl's father and the surgeon, still in his theatre scrubs, regarded the small, anaesthetised child in the framed bed. Each man locked in his private thoughts.

'Thank you, I know you've done all you could.' Andrew Bannister's voice cracked as he squeezed the surgeon's arm gently and then allowed himself to be ushered from the room.

From there he headed back to the children's recovery ward to comfort his other daughter and son who lay in adjacent beds, bruised and bandaged.

'How's Georgie, Dad?' they asked in unison.

'She's doing fine. Try and get some sleep now and do your best not to worry – you're all going to be fine.' With that Andrew bent over and kissed each of them on the forehead before leaving the room.

'Mr Bannister?'
Andrew looked up from his desk to see two traffic policemen standing in the open farm office door. 'Yes, how can I help you?'
'I'm afraid your wife has been involved in a fatal accident.'
The word 'fatal' sliced through him.

Georgie's sleep was restless as she struggled unconsciously with the hospital security bands in place to limit her movement. Her lips moved and occasionally she let out a whimper; in between times she called for her mother.

In her many and varied dreams, she heard a loud explosion. People were screaming. Later the deafening sound of an engine. The bright sun above was splintered by the spokes of a spinning wheel.

Then she was on a high cliff top and Jason the horrible boy in her class was pushing her off the edge. She grabbed at air and found a large multi-coloured umbrella in her hand and started to float like the lady in the film. Down, down she went. There seemed no end to her descent. The sea below was blue-grey and menacing; the white-tipped waves appeared like fingers of huge hands trying to grasp her and pull her below to hidden depths.

The umbrella started to save her and slow her descent. There were soft voices and ladies singing. Everything was becoming brighter. A huge shining light seemed to be directed towards her. An old, bearded man waved to her from behind the light as she continued her flight.

Now she was surrounded by beautiful white doves with green fronds in their beaks weaving this way and that around her. They appeared to be guiding her and she became even more alarmed as she couldn't work out how to steer the course of the umbrella.

Her fears increased. She heard her daddy's voice calling her.

'Georgie, Georgie.' She felt drops of water. She opened her eyes. His head was above her, and beyond his smiling face streaked with tears she saw two doves painted on the hospital ceiling.

Dinner for One

Glove between his teeth, James fumbled with his door key while trying not to lose his grip on the Tesco Bag for Life. The blasted key fought against going home. The phone continued to ring. He was very close to tears.

By the time he managed to turn the key and squeeze past the artificial Christmas tree the phone had stopped ringing. He put the 'special offer' of champagne and truffles in the fridge, checked the turkey crown in the oven, then switched on the answer machine. Angela's voice crackled, 'Sorry love 'fraid I can't make it.'

Not another year!

Dorset Blue Vinney

'Excuse me miss.' It was the red-faced man on table twelve with the extremely thin wife.

'Yes sir, can I help you?' Laura was dreading this; her second evening in the restaurant of a small family hotel in Swanage. Instinctively she knew this spelt trouble.

'What type of cheese is this?' he asked somewhat rudely, pointing at his cheese platter with his knife as though it was some toxic substance.

'I believe it is Blue Vinney, sir,' she replied hoping to God that it really was.

'But I distinctly asked for Stilton.' His irritation stepped up a level while his wife looked embarrassed as other diners were now paying attention to the situation.

'Oh, that's right', Laura countered regaining her confidence. 'The chef said that we did not have any Stilton sir, and that Blue Vinney is very similar but better. It is locally produced here in Dorset.'

'Surely if I asked for Stilton it would mean I wanted Stilton wouldn't it? And, if you didn't have any and chose to serve your own make, doesn't it behove you to at least tell me. Wouldn't you agree?' Laura just stood and stared, her face turning pink; she could sense tears forming.

He continued glaring at Laura. His wife muttered something unintelligible and was silenced by his outstretched hand. She began to look even more uncomfortable.

'Excuse me,' it was the man from the next table, a lone diner, 'I take it you are not from these parts?'

'What's it to you?' He turned to face this new intervention that had been addressed by an elderly man in a wheelchair.

'Well nothing really, I just wondered whether anyone being as inconsiderate as you, had grown up in this town. You see I am also a visitor and found the staff here, in particular the young lady serving you, so helpful, and was thus curious. That's all.' With that he returned to reading the book he had opened next to his plate.

The red-faced man's face became even redder. Laura continued standing on the spot searching her brain, but her inexperience overcame her thinking ability. She just couldn't think of any further excuse and her feet felt welded to the spot. The man's wife now seemed to be looking for somewhere to hide, when all of a sudden her husband stood up. Shoving his chair aside he made as if to leave the room. He got three steps from the table when he collapsed to the floor with an almost imperceptible thud.

The next few moments were a blur of people rushing to the man's side; many cries of 'How awful.' Both Laura and the man's wife burst into tears.

Unexpectedly a man from table six stood up, announced he was a doctor, and kneeling beside the fallen figure loosened his tie and proceeded to apply mouth to mouth resuscitation, without success.

The manager called through the doorway that an ambulance was on its way. Fifteen minutes later two paramedics appeared in the room and said, 'What seems to be the problem?'

The gentleman in the wheelchair looked up and said, 'Dorset Blue Vinney.'

The Price of Magic

At the end of a long, hot February day in 1967 my driver and I were bouncing along a country road in Eastern Nigeria, shortly to be renamed Biafra if the rumours on the bush telegraph were true. Perhaps, if I had I not been dozing as we entered the village that afternoon, I might have noticed the distinct absence of people. But I was tired, half asleep and not really paying any attention.

Usually, this large village would be peppered with the inhabitants going about their basic daily tasks of life in rural West Africa. Life was easy for the men; little bothered them, huddled in small groups gossiping, offering pearls of wisdom about a myriad of subjects they enjoyed speculating about. When or if General Jack Gowon's federal army would attack Ojukwu's Enugu headquarters, the lack of yams this year or maybe just the price of palm wine. Opinions are free and the time to express them endless.

Under the shade of trees in between the houses their wives would be squatting, working over rough wooden mortars pounding the ingredients for the evening meal with long wooden pestles, thrusting them down onto yellow yams with a one-handed easy motion that years of practice brought.

Young boys would also have an easy time playing barefoot soccer on the grounds of the Catholic school. But for women and young girls life was more arduous, sashaying along the edges of the roads balancing plastic buckets or tall square tins on their heads, filled with water from the local river. Carriers in the neverending job of water supply to homes that lacked even that basic facility. This was their evening task, the mornings would be taken up tending cassava crops or collecting firewood.

But today there was no-one in sight. Being half asleep this simply didn't register until Godwin, sensing my stirring, said 'Must be big Juju party today Masta.'

'What makes you think that?' I yelled back irritably in an attempt to compete with the combined noise of the Land Rover's throbbing diesel engine and the crashing and banging of the vehicle thumping into the ruts and potholes of the poorly maintained laterite road.

'All people gone, sir – must be go to village meeting place.' This brought a smile to his face because it enabled him to show me just how much more knowledgeable he was of all things Nigerian.

Further along we encountered occasional individuals and then small groups, all heading into the village centre. Rounding a slow curve running to the right ahead of us, I could see what appeared to be a tumultuous crowd amassed right across the town; there must have been hundreds, possibly thousands. Some men turned out in what must be their Sunday best, soft Trilby hats or traditional bright coloured caps. A small number of the ladies wore bright coloured cotton national dress with matching headgear; the majority were less well-off and dressed more simply. A sprinkling of green and yellow umbrellas advertising Star Beer stood out amongst the crowd like lilies in a pond. I could now hear the sound of highlife music coming from taxi-trucks playing this through roof-mounted loudspeakers to attract customers or simply attention.

Godwin slowed to a crawl and in a few moments we were up against the back edge of the crowd. Realising our arrival, the nearest turned and stared, first at the vehicle and then at me. Godwin had no option other than to stop. The sea of people in front of us covered the entire area. Several school children slipped out from the crowd and gathered round us – in a poor country area with little to amuse them a white face showing up is a welcome distraction. They whispered loudly 'Oyibo' meaning white person, and giggled.

'Is there another way round this place Godwin?' By now I was starting to become more than a little anxious at the size of the crowd, feeling we could be stuck here for hours, and I didn't fancy travelling home in the dark; road conditions in daylight are scary but at night the dangers increase exponentially.

'No sir, this is the only way, no other road because river and swamp.' Godwin's voice was much quieter now, not simply because he didn't have to compete with the noise of the vehicle as we were stopped, but our conversation was no longer private as the children were so close, one with his head stuck through Godwin's side window poking his tongue out at me, before being swatted away by Godwin.

'Well, if this is the only way let's start moving, just nudge them a little; I'm sure they will move.' I endeavoured to sound more confident than I felt.

He engaged first gear and started to move forward gingerly, sounding the horn, his face tightened into a grimace and he broke out in a sweat with the concentration of obeying my order. Those directly in our path half turned and moved to one side, stumbling over one another in an attempt to let us through. Some didn't budge until the bumper bar actually touched them. Very soon the vehicle became completely engulfed in a sea of bodies. As the ones in front moved to allow us passage so they closed up behind us. Soon we were surrounded. It really was quite frightening.

Few, apart from the children, had any interest in us other than getting out of our way. Everyone was craning to see something up ahead. Whatever it was, it seemed more important that the risk of being run over. I wasn't sure who was sweating the most, Godwin or me. By now the nuisance of delay had been pushed into second place. Fear was in first place, by some measure.

Our progress could be calculated in people sliding slowly by either side of us. We made about twenty metres and suddenly a hush went through the crowd. Without warning a Juju man in a hideous ebony mask fringed with dried grass leaped onto the spare tyre on the bonnet. Godwin stalled the motor. The man was well built and the bare parts of his flesh were smeared with white paint. Over the natural colour of his black skin it produced an eerie grey appearance, as though he had recently rolled in the ashes of a fire. The rest of his clothing was crudely fashioned out of old sackcloth with various small effigies and bones dangling from it. In his hand, a cudgel with a carved wooden skull on the end and in the other hand some kind of rattle that he banged on my side of the windscreen and in clear English shouted, 'Give me five pounds.'

Godwin's eyes looked like they would pop out of his head. He was visibly shaking like a man in the throes of a fever.

The Juju man screamed again, 'Give me five pounds.' And shook the rattle.

'No way will I give you five pounds. Start moving Godwin.'

'Mr John, please sir we cannot until you pay him. I will pay you back sir, if you just give him the five pounds.' I should point out here that Godwin's salary was about five shillings a day.

'Look Godwin, this is just an ordinary bloke, just like you and me, well rather more like you actually, and I'm buggered if I will give him five pounds from either your pocket or mine, so please move forward so we can get out of this place.'

'No, Mr John, sir, I beg you please give him the money,' Godwin turned to face me, pleading, close to tears by now. Realising something had to give I fished in my pocket and came up with about twelve shillings in change.

I put my arm around the left hand side of the vehicle with the coins in my hand and offered it to the Juju man.

'Here take this, sorry it's all I have I'm afraid,' lying as convincingly as I could and decorating it with a forced smile. He looked at the money, then at me for what seemed an eternity, and then as quick as lightning he snatched the money and disappeared as though he had never been there and was simply a figment of my imagination.

'Perhaps you'll be good enough to start moving forward again Godwin. This time give 'em a bit more horn. I think we're late enough as it is. Magic is cheaper than you think.'

My fears had now changed to worrying if I could get out of the town with dry, unsoiled shorts.

Caspian Days

Maryam lay wide awake; it was one-thirty in the morning. It was always this time of the year - midsummer - when her bedroom became too warm and she had trouble sleeping. At 25 years of age she still lived with her parents, as she remained unmarried. They kept telling her she was still young and beautiful, but she knew that with the way her father ruled the family and the scarcity of suitable bachelors, it was extremely unlikely she would find a husband.

It wasn't simply the heat that woke her. It was that dream again. The one about the encounter in her early childhood while on a family evacuation from the war. Normally it was the habit of her father to move the family to their house they owned by the Caspian Sea to avoid the summer heat of Tehran. That year it was to avoid the danger of Iraqi missiles as well.

She was only eight years old at that time and free to roam alone in the early mornings without the need to be accompanied by her brothers. This particular morning she had gone down to the beach just along from their house while the family stayed sleeping after the late party the previous night. It was so refreshing after the stuffy confines of her bedroom, skipping along the sand and wading in the sea.

As she progressed further along the shoreline she spotted a bright blue dinghy pulled up on the beach so she ran towards it and climbed inside. It was such fun sitting in the bow like a boatman, pretending she was at sea, placing her hand above her eye-line scanning the horizon.

But her game was interrupted by the sound of a dog barking just behind her. Afraid she would be discovered, she instinctively crouched down and peered over the rim. She saw the dog alongside a shepherd-boy, who was starting to undress only a few metres away, unaware of her presence.

The whiteness of his body contrasted with his sunburnt arms and face as he stripped completely. Maryam had never seen a naked boy. She marvelled at how different his body was to hers. Once undressed, he ran and dived into the surf; Maryam clambered out of the boat and ran for home.

It was the only time she was to see a male form. The Ayatollah's obsession with the war against Saddam Hussein had taken thousands of young men and boys she might have known, perhaps married.

Her one surviving brother had married and had his own family, but she had no proposals, no marriage and only this dream.

A Bridge Over Troubled Waters

As I turned the corner and climbed the pavement leading up to the bridge over the river, a figure caught my eye. Though my mind was on other matters, I instantly recognised the young waitress who only a couple of hours before had served my lunch in the hotel restaurant.

I could have sworn she was attempting to hoist herself onto the bridge wall but stopped when she saw me, dropped back to the pavement and just stared ahead along the river.

'Hello – are you okay?' I ventured, unsure if I should intervene, worried I could be wrong, and my approach rebuked.

'I'm okay thanks – you startled me that's all,' she glanced briefly in my direction before turning back to the river. I think I caught a hint of an eastern European accent, but I couldn't be sure, as she spoke so softly.

She was slight, with blonde hair fashioned in a ponytail just as in the restaurant. No longer wearing her uniform, she was dressed in jeans and a faded red hoodie. The strangest thing was she did not have any shoes on, odd in mid-October.

'Are you sure? It looked to me as though you were trying to climb on to the wall. Where on earth are your shoes? Aren't your feet cold?'

'Really I'm okay – please leave me alone – please.' She wasn't rude, just sad and pleading. I was tempted to acquiesce, but something said I should persist.

'Look I'm sorry if you think I'm being nosy, but I think if we got off this bridge and had a chat I might be of some help.'

This last remark seemed as though it sliced through her control, and she sank to a crouch position rather like a marionette would collapse when the puppeteer drops the strings. She clutched her face in her hands and muttered through them 'Why couldn't you just leave me alone?'

'I suppose I could but I'm sure you've noticed I am a priest and I apologise for interfering; you see I am obliged to offer help even when, as it appears, it is not welcome. Come, I'm sure we can find some solution to your problems.' By now I was beginning to worry how this might appear to a passer-by but thankfully the place was quite quiet.

As circumstances stood my thoughts were as much for myself as for this poor unfortunate young woman, and in all honesty it might be better if we linked hands and jumped together. I quickly banished the thought.

I was on my way to an interview with the Bishop that could well spell the end of my career. The misinterpretation of this situation with a young girl crouched as if in fear of me could easily tip the balance of the scales of my future, already in serious jeopardy.

'Get off her you bastard!' I turned just in time to receive a painful blow to my left jaw that sent me sprawling over the crouching girl onto the pavement beyond her, catching my elbow against the stone wall and knocking off my glasses.

My assailant, as far as I could make out without my glasses, had a bushy beard and was wearing black and white check trousers; the sort favoured by professional chefs.

'Come on Alicia let's get away from this pervert. As for you mate you ain't 'eard the last of this.'

Before I could say a word they were gone and I was abandoned on the pavement searching for my glasses.

The Bangkok Bash

'Patpong Road Mr Gary, or straight home?' My driver Noi seemed to know my habits better than me these days.

'No, thanks, Noi. I reckon I've had enough for one night. Straight home and put your foot down.' Normally I would have gone down to Patpong to one of the many bars there.

But it was December 23rd and the night of our staff Christmas party at the Australian Embassy. The Poms pride themselves on being able to do the pageantry bit, but I reckon we put on the best Christmas bash amongst the embassies here. You'd think the Yanks would outdo us, but they had become a bit too nervous about recent terrorist scares to put on too big a splash or invite outsiders.

Noi pulled out into the usual busy night-time traffic and I prepared myself for a little snooze on the way home. I lived a fair way up Sukumvit Road, not far as the crow flies, but at least half an hour in this traffic.

'Good party Mr Gary?' Noi asked into his rear-view mirror. 'Sure was, Noi. That's why I think it would be better to go straight home as I expect Lek will be more than a little pissed off that I'm this late, especially as she didn't come to the party.'

Lek was my regular girlfriend. We had been going steady for a while now. She worked in the Central Department Store; we met one Saturday when I was shopping there. She was a super girl but a bit out of her depth when it came to social occasions at the embassy. For that reason I decided to go on my own, which didn't go down too well.

I flopped back into the air-conditioned comfort of the car and looked out of the side window. The next thing I knew Noi was tapping me on the arm.

'Jesus, what time is it? I must have died.'

'It's two-thirty Mr Gary, traffic was okay tonight, only take bit over half an hour.'

The house was in complete darkness which was very odd seeing as Lek was staying over, and if for some reason she wasn't, the maid would have left the outside lights on before she left.

'Must be a power failure?'

'No sir,' Noi said, 'Look, house next door still got lights on.'

He was right, their lights were on alright, but my compound was in complete darkness.

I'd just got out of the car and trying to adjust my vision when all of a sudden a figure loomed out of the shadows gabbling on in Thai. To my relief it was only the watchman.

'Jesus, Suporn, you scared the shit out of me! What the bloody hell are you doing skulking about in the shadows, and why are the lights off?' These conversations happen regularly, which was totally stupid on my part as neither of us understood a word spoken between us. It required Noi to take on the role of translator as well as diplomat to calm me down, as my temper got the better of me.

'He say sorry, Mr Gary, he doesn't know why there's no lights. Maybe Miss Lek turned them off by mistake. He also say he sorry he frightened you but batteries in his flashlight have finished. He say he told you yesterday.'

'Alright, alright, I'll sort it out. You bugger off home, Noi. Come back at ten, I want to do a bit of shopping as I think some extra Christmas presents might be needed.'

'Okay, sir, goodnight,' and with that he was off.

Gingerly I felt my way along the path from the drive to the front door. My eyes had adjusted themselves a little by now as I reached the front door, felt for the keyhole and unlocked it.

I quietly stepped inside and shut the door behind me. Once inside it seemed even darker and I cursed as I banged my shin on something heavy as I struggled to find the light switch. Recovering my balance, I found it and turned them on, then as I bent down to take my shoes off, a figure leapt out of the shadow of the bookcase and jumped on me. For the second time in a matter of minutes I was scared out of my wits until I realised from the perfume that it was Lek.

'What the bloody hell are you doing you silly cow?'

43

I did my best to shake her off, but it was very difficult to defend myself without hurting her; consequently, she scratched my right cheek before I could grab her wrists.

'You are bad, bad man Gary,' she screamed in my ear as the pair of us fell to the floor. 'Why you leave me at home? Are you ashamed of me? What have I done? Have you been with some bar girl? My momma say you are butterfly.'

She was completely hysterical; I'd never seen her like this before.

'Look, I'll let you go if you can just control yourself,' I yelled. By now I was on my knees holding her by the wrists and she was half lying, in front of me.

I started to get up and let go of her, but she renewed her attack and flew at me again. Dodging her flailing hands, I grappled her to the ground again. I could taste the blood trickling down my cheek. With the shock and the amount of Christmas grog inside me, I was close to throwing up, and would if this went on much longer.

Through the fog of alcohol I had an inspiration. God knows why I suddenly thought of it. When I was a kid visiting my granddad's farm, his old cockerel attacked me. The second time it happened, granddad was watching and he simply grabbed it by the legs, whirled it round and round above his head and tossed it into the corner of the yard. The bird tried to stand up but fell over twice before it made off looking very sorry for itself.

'That's how you deal with a stroppy chook, young feller, and works every time.' I never forgot the lesson.

That's what I needed to do to calm Lek down. I grabbed her ankles, got to my feet and started to whirl her around. This'll do the trick if nothing does.

'Garree....' she screamed, 'Put me down please.'

But I kept on spinning, just like granddad did with the cockerel. On about the second rotation I got a bit giddy and almost dropped her and then there was a sickening thud. Her head must have banged against the heavy bookcase. The pair of us crashed to the floor again.

'Oh Jesus! I've killed her, I've bloody killed her.'

She just lay there completely lifeless. There was a cut on her forehead and a trickle of blood was oozing from it. I could see tomorrow's headlines in the Bangkok Post – 'Australian diplomat kills Thai beauty.' This could be the end of my bloody career. Everything I'd worked for. It would be the worst scandal the embassy had ever faced. I'd be lucky if they gave me life. More likely, it would be execution by firing squad.

What a stupid, stupid bastard, what have I done? In an attempt to calm myself I tried to think as rationally as possible what to do next. I need to get her out of here and quick. I straightened out the rug that had become rucked up, dragged her by the ankles alongside it and rolled her up in it.

Now to get her to the car and dump her somewhere; my mind was racing. Of course, that silly bugger Suporn will be hanging around out there, just when I don't want him to be. I'll need to get rid of him while I put her in the boot.

I opened the door and went outside, closing it behind me. 'Suporn,' I yelled into the yard, and he appeared out of the shadows. I gave him a thousand baht note and ordered 'Beer Singha, Beer Singha, nung carton.' I made the shape of a box with my arms. He looked at me as though I was mad. He had undertaken this simple task many times before, but perhaps never at three in the morning.

'Go on you dopey sod, get me beer.' He took the money and headed for the gates. Once he was gone I quickly opened the boot of the car. Thank God it was empty, need to move fast.

I rushed back into the house and with a supreme effort hoisted the wrapped-up body over my shoulder. Thank goodness Thais are so light. I couldn't do this with one of the Sheilas back home. I staggered through the front door, put the bundle into the boot and closed the lid.

I leaned against the side of the car to catch my breath. I looked in the glove compartment for the car keys where Noi always left them. No sooner had I found them than bloody Suporn was back lugging a case of beer with a grin on his face like a fox eating chicken guts in long grass.

I couldn't believe it. If I'd been dying for a beer, he would have been gone for hours. I just stood staring at him. He motioned with his chin, should he carry the beer into the house. I shook my head. He mustn't see the mess inside. Because I didn't want the beer in the house he supposed I wanted it in the car and started moving towards the boot. I overtook him and tried to wrestle the case from him, but the stupid sod resisted in some dumb servile desire to complete his task.

While all this was going on I felt I was within a hair's breadth of heart failure or throwing up, or both. Then a dull thudding sound came from the boot of the car, followed by Lek's muffled cries, clearly audible in the still of the night.

'Help! Help! Someone help, please.'

We were married three weeks later in a church in Convent Road. My parents and sister came up from Brisbane and the whole embassy turned out. We would have got married on New Year's Day, but we had to wait until the bruise on Lek's forehead faded a bit.

A Lost Lover

Rosie Walsh lay back in her easy chair basking in a warming shaft of April sunshine through the side window. Having just had her elevenses of coffee made with milk, and two chocolate digestives, she was feeling relaxed and ready for a small nap before lunch.

'You alright in there, Rose?' Her carer poked her head around the door and was pleased to see that the old girl was fast asleep in her chair. The steady rise and fall of her cardigan assured her all was well.

Rose slept soundly, dreaming of days gone by when Albert first called to take her out. Course she was Rose Edwards then and everybody called her Rosie even though it was in fact her second name. She was really Nellie Rose Edwards, the same as her grandmother, but she couldn't stand Nellie. Her main objection to it was that the boy next door, Frank Kimber, always used to sing 'Nellie put your belly next to mine' whenever he saw her.

She hated that boy Kimber almost as much as she loved Albert, yet it was strange how she always dreamt about both of them in equal amounts. Funny really because she had been married to Roger Walsh right up to his death and hadn't seen neither hide nor hair of the other two in donkey's years.

She did have one disturbing dream where the Queen Mother made a visit to the town and met Roger pushing Margaret's pram up the High Street, and he told her it wasn't his baby.

It was the war that messed her life up. She and Albert were going steady when he got his papers and was shipped off first to Aldershot and then to North Africa. Two months later she discovered she was pregnant. He was sunning himself by the Suez Canal and she was trying her best not to let her parents hear her being sick in the toilet.

Though she never particularly liked the family butcher's son Roger, she knew he carried a torch for her and she was desperate.

Within six weeks of returning his smiles they were married quietly in the local church.

A few tongues wagged behind her back. She was well aware that nobody believed she was four months early when her daughter Margaret Rose was born. She never knew whether her husband ever realised the baby was not his, right up until the day he died.

As the years slipped by, the question of who was Margaret's father was never queried until Albert was demobbed at the end of the war. They met in the recreation ground one Tuesday morning as she was sat watching the child on the swings.

She almost fainted when Albert put his hand on her shoulder and said, 'Hello Rosie, you're looking well.' She hadn't seen him approaching

Her face first went shock white and then bright red. Words failed her and she looked up and down the park to make sure there were no witnesses to the meeting. Margaret continued swinging, lost in her own little world while her mother fought back tears at the sight of the man in army uniform who was her father.

Rose continued her silence and Albert said, 'I've been watching the little girl on the swings. She's mine, isn't she?' Before she had chance to reply he turned on his heel and left as quickly as he had appeared. She was going to call out for him to stop. She could explain. The words wouldn't come, but quiet tears did and rolled down her cheeks. The cheeks that were crimson with embarrassment, shame and sorrow all mixed into one.

She walked Margaret often to the recreation ground in the vain hope that he might try and find her again after that brief encounter, but he never did. She found out he had left the town the next day and she later learned he had emigrated to New Zealand.

She and Roger never had any more children; it wasn't for lack of trying on his part, and she was more than a little relieved when he took up bowling and seemed to lose interest in trying to make a friend for Margaret.

Roger actually died at the bowling green. It was a grudge match against their main rivals from the next town and he missed on his last bowl. It would have won them the match and the trophy but he missed by a whisker. They told Rose the disappointment had hit him so hard he'd simply rolled over from the kneeling position and died of a massive stroke.

The whole club turned out to his funeral, and many of the townsfolk, as the last surviving family member of Walsh's butchers he was well known and liked in equal measures. Margaret, her husband and two sons escorted Rose to the funeral, and they gave him a good send-off. She felt confused but really not truly sad. He was a good man, a loving father to her child, and she never wanted for anything throughout their married life. But like is not love.

She survived him by fifteen years, living alone in the family home until Margaret persuaded her to go into the retirement home. At first, she didn't want to, but she was glad that she had done so. She was able to chat to both residents and staff and it stopped her thoughts returning to Albert all those years ago. Strange as it might seem, Roger's death somehow released her from having to be grateful to a man she really didn't love.

Noon came and Rose slept on. The carer came calling along the hall: 'Mrs Walsh, Rosie, there's a call for you. Says he knows you well, sounds a bit like an Australian, Rosie.'

But she couldn't wake her, then or ever.

A Good Time to Disappear

'C'mon Lori for heaven's sake, wake up, will you? I told you not to get so pissed last night cos we had this trip booked this morning. Get up and get bloody dressed or we're going to miss the boat.'

'Leave me alone. I don't want to go on any bloody boat trip.'

'But we've paid for it Lori.' Katy was getting angry now as she knew her friend could be really lazy and stubborn at times like this. She had witnessed it so many times in the past.

'So what? Tell 'em I'm sick or something. You're pretty good at excuses.' Lori pulled the pillow over her head as she rolled away from Katy.

'Alright that's it. I'm never ever going with you on holiday again, Lori Chalmers. You've been nothing but a pain in the arse since we left home, and this is the last straw.' With that Katy picked up her bag and stormed out of the room slamming the door behind her.

The two girls had arranged this trip to New Zealand at the last minute. Katy only came to accompany Lori to get her out of this huge well of depression she had fallen into when her boyfriend Danny unceremoniously dumped her on her birthday.

The trip was an all-in last-minute deal and covered a four week tour of New Zealand. They had just explored the volcanoes around Rotorua when a tout suggested the trip to White Island to see the famous volcano out there.

Having managed to get back to sleep for a few hours Lori staggered out of bed and headed for the bathroom. She was desperate for the toilet. Sitting on the toilet she mulled over the thoughts most prominent in her state of alcoholic depression. She flushed the toilet, walked back into the room, switched on the television and fell back on the bed.

On the television two significant things caused her to sit up and gasp loudly. The first were the huge plumes of smoke emitting from what the television presenter said was White Island. The second was the time. She had been asleep for five hours since Katy left.

'Jesus!' was all she could exclaim through the fingers of the hand clasped over her mouth. Having watched and listened to the report of the catastrophe that had occurred at the site where Katy was and where she herself should have been, tears sprung into her eyes.

Minutes later, standing under the welcome relief of the shower, a plan started to formulate in her mind. Everyone would think she was caught up in that disaster. Just like some of those people she read about in the papers covering the tower block fire in London. She was going to disappear.

It was time for a change. Wipe out the miseries of her past life and start afresh. She started to hum as she completed her shower. She had a lot to do.

When the Sun Came Up Like Thunder from Kalimantan

It was so rewarding to meet up for a few drinks with the section and enjoy one of Janet's hearty lamb stews.

Teddy, Janet's husband, had arranged the whole day for me. First a visit to the village churchyard for Janet and me to pay our respects at our parent's grave. As we did every December 21 since our mum joined dad there. That it coincided with the night of the attack was eerie, if not downright weird. Memories.

Sarawak, Borneo, December 20, 1965. It was my first real leadership test with a shiny new pip on my shoulder. But of course, I wasn't wearing it there. I cannot really claim that it was under my leadership because without Sergeant McLaughlin I would have been lost, both literally and for real. Between us, we led the first section of Charlie Platoon that day.

The first time I really got to know Neal McLaughlin was when we travelled across the Causeway from Singapore over to the jungle training camp in Johore Bahru. I can't say I wasn't excited because I was. But I was also nervous, never having been in a jungle before.

It was there we learned various new skills shown by a Malay sergeant whose faded and starched uniform made us all look so amateurish when compared to our brand new, jungle-greens, especially with our pale skins straight from an English climate. We were also introduced to the most feared creature after snakes. Leeches. How detestable they were, especially if one got on you undetected at night and grew bloated on your blood.

First job was to sharpen our goloks, the army issue machete, and cut branches to construct bashers, a crude tent made with two groundsheets in which we slept in pairs. McLaughlin took to it as though he had grown up in the woods when in fact, he was from the Gorbals in Glasgow. He and I shared our first basher. How he managed to sleep so soundly astounded me. I woke up with every rustle, imagining all sorts of creatures.

After two whole days at the school we were considered fully trained to survive life in the jungle. A week later we were shipped across the South China Sea and up the river into the city of Kuching. The sights, smells and sounds of the Orient were everything I imagined after reading Conrad.

But Kuching wasn't for the likes of us. We were destined for the 'Ulu' – the jungle – and a couple of days later we were taken there. First by truck as far as the road went and then by helicopters into our base overlooking the enemy, President Sukarno's Indonesian Borneo, Kalimantan. Here we learned many more skills in the art of jungle fighting and survival.

The camp was a series of five-foot deep trenches connecting sleeping bunks. They ran around the hilltop as though some giant monster worm had burrowed endlessly and then had his lair exposed. In the centre was a helicopter pad on which our supplies arrived.

During the days we spent what spare time we had writing letters home. We exercised or played volleyball on the helipad depending on availability. Every morning I attended various 'O' groups with the Officer Commanding for daily briefings and the planning of attacks against our enemy across the border.

The plan was to walk in four separate sections along individual routes during the day, hopefully undetected, and make camp ready for a dawn raid. Operation Sparrow Fart. The trek through the rainforest that day was exhausting and scary. I imagined an enemy behind every tree and clump of bamboo. We marched in absolute silence. The only sounds came from birds and the screeches of monkeys above our heads, every one of them sending my jangling nerves even more on edge.

We made camp just before dusk in the knowledge that we were now well and truly in enemy territory. Everyone worked in an unnatural silence. Nerves continued to be the order of the day. I don't think any of us slept that night; even McLaughlin was restless.

Just as we were collecting ourselves together and the sun started to rise and shine dimly through the bush, the sky burst into light. The tables were turned; we the attackers were being ambushed. There were several deafening explosions all around us. That was the last I remembered of that day and that mission, and of my short-lived army service.

I knew nothing of my return journey. Apparently, I was stretchered for half a day until it was safe to prepare a helicopter pad. The RAF did the rest, straight back to Kuching. Do not stop. Return to go. In this case a hospital in East Grinstead in dear old Blighty.

Now here we are ten years on from that fateful day. Waiting for the doorbell to ring at Teddy and Janet's farmhouse. When it rings Teddy will see them in because I can't. Can't see, that is.

But I can hug each one of the five or six who managed to make it here today, shepherded by Sergeant Major McLaughlin MC. If only I could see their friendly faces. Ah well, you can't have it all I suppose. I have learned to make do with touch.

A Seven Letter Word

'You know I'm meeting Angela this morning darling?' Jane was
talking to her husband Harvey while applying lipstick with the aid of
the lounge mirror and watching for his reaction from his armchair
across the room.

'Are you? Can't say as I remember, not that it's a problem.' He
looked up from his paper where he had been tackling his daily
crossword with moderate success. His wife said that in his case
crossword had a double meaning in that he invariably became
irritable with whomsoever the compiler was, especially on
Thursdays.

'The trouble is you never do remember darling, but I should be
back by dinnertime and I have done all the prep. So we will eat on
time if that's what bothering you.' She finished applying the lipstick,
turned side on to the mirror, smoothed the back of her recently dyed
hair and then turned to smile at Harvey who was oblivious to this
attempt at remote affection. He was still trying to answer a very
simple clue that he was sure had appeared before, but he was damned
if he could remember. It really was so frustrating when solutions
kept buzzing around in his mind but defied retrieval. He was certain
he knew the answer, but it continued to elude him. 'A summer bird
in adverse weather conditions' – seven letters.

'Right, I'm off. You'll be able to find something suitable for a
sandwich in the fridge darling; see you later.' She blew him a kiss
that landed in a similar place to the smile earlier as he continued to
do battle with the crossword.

'Yep, okay, say hello to Angela from me,' but his words simply
hit the inside of the front door as Jane had already closed it behind
her and was fishing for the remote control for the garage door in her
handbag.

As the crosswords in Harvey's life went, this wasn't too bad and
by a quarter to twelve he had finished it all except for two connecting

words; one up and one down, and if nothing else he knew when he was stumped. He prided himself at not being a quitter, but enough was enough and once he left it alone the answer would come to him later in the day. It nearly always did.

He continued reading the rest of his newspaper. The phone rang. He ignored it, knowing it would either be for Jane or some charlatan from the sub-continent wanting him to inadvertently divulge information that might lead to his financial disadvantage, while pretending to help him with a non-existent computer virus. Whoever it was they didn't leave a message on the answering machine, so he felt vindicated.

Strange really that Jane had managed to get him to ignore phone calls. Back in his working life he wouldn't dream of ignoring a call even though there were times when he wished he had. His decision was influenced by the fact that so many of his calls to Jane when he was overseas went unanswered, and she admitted she was in at the time but thought it was probably a cold caller.

There was a period towards the latter part of his working life, when overseas trips became more frequent and lasted longer, that the unanswered phone calls played on his mind in spite of Jane's explanation. That and the fact that he sensed they were growing apart and didn't share the same likes and dislikes anymore. He often felt that they would have had more in common if they had had children, but they didn't, and somehow neither of them was able to discuss this fact.

Many a time he mulled it over in his mind to bring it into a conversation in their early married life, but every time he lacked the courage, fearing that it was a taboo subject. He was afraid that she would interpret the lack as her fault when in actual fact it had never been established whose fault it was, as they had never sought medical advice.

Having finished with the paper, and somewhat at a loss as how he should spend the rest of the day, he phoned his friend Patrick to see if he fancied a pint and a sandwich. His call went unanswered, so he decided to go out anyway. It was definitely preferable to sitting around the house. Moreover, he decided to treat himself to the new lunchtime special they were advertising at the hotel in town. At least the prospect of dining alone never bothered him greatly, as he had plenty of experience in doing so. The prospect of the visit into town began to please him, so he decided to make an effort in his attire by changing his trousers for a smart pair of silver-grey corduroys and putting on a tie, something he rarely did in the daytime since retiring.

The journey into town took a little longer than normal as he indulged himself further by going the pretty way. He parked in the central car park and stopped off on the walk to the hotel to buy a magazine in the newsagents off the square. It was just a current affairs weekly that would compensate for the lack of conversation during his lunch. In the past he would eliminate the silence at meal times alone by reading novels. He was particularly fond of spy stories, especially those written by le Carré. But since retiring he found he had lost the appetite to tackle anything of length, even though he now had plenty of time to do so. He put it down to his reading a daily newspaper, struggling with crosswords, listening to the radio and of course the biggest waster of all time, television. He often wondered to himself where the time disappeared to.

Entering the hotel, he was just about to turn into the dining room when, glancing along the corridor leading into the bar, he saw Patrick engaged in conversation. The person he was talking to was obscured by the narrowness of the corridor so he decided he would at least go and say hello. As he walked further along the corridor the legs and dress of Patrick's guest came into view just before he announced his arrival.

An icy chill ran through his body as he recognised who it was and he turned around. Quickly walking away, he turned into the lobby and headed for the restrooms. He was in a blind panic as he shoved open the swing door, failing to see the small yellow sandwich-board warning that the floor was wet. His feet went from under him: his only thought before his head cracked on the porcelain washbasin was the one word across, he had not finished. Cuckold.

At a little after six o'clock Jane entered the house and called out 'I've left the car in the driveway darling as I might go out early tomorrow.' There was no answer, and just as she noticed how strange it was that Harvey had not put any lights on, she saw the little red light blinking on the answering machine.

Holiday in Mogadishu

In late November 1992 I was assigned to travel from Cairo, where I was resident, to Ethiopia to make a scouting trip in the Ogaden, a region in the Horn of Africa, for a potential seismic contract.

Arriving in Addis Ababa I checked into the Hilton Hotel where I was to meet up with the personnel from the oil company. Ethiopia was far from what I had expected. Like most people, I suppose, the only images of the country I had seen was via the media in the run up to Geldof's 'Live Aid' in the mid-eighties. I fully expected flat desert lands, not the green hills and mountains around Addis that I saw from the plane as we prepared to land.

The Hilton Hotel itself boasted natural hot springs in the gardens surrounding the swimming pool. The majority of the guests, it seemed, were from a variety of international charity and aid organisations. From early evening to late into the night the bar hummed with talk of all that was being achieved to help Ethiopia out of its basket-case status. I've never been a fan of NGO personnel even though I have met some interesting individuals from time to time. To be surrounded by such a gaggle of well-fed westerners filling their bellies with local beer in a five-star hotel did little to alter my opinion.

The next morning I checked the hotel reception desk for the leader of my clients, and found them in the restaurant having breakfast. The group comprised of three Americans, Reggie, the leader and exploration manager, Herman, a geologist and Tom, a geophysicist. We were hosted by a resident geologist with the World Bank, an American called Bill, who was the mastermind of this oil exploration project.

Over the next couple of weeks, I came to know these four characters quite well. Reggie was a dashing mixed-race young man with the looks of Johnny Mathis. He was extremely enthusiastic and seemed to fall in love with every Ethiopian he met. Herman was short, bespectacled and gave the impression of being quite bookish. Tom on the other hand was what would best be described as 'a good old boy' whose most noticeable physical feature was a poorly matching hairpiece. He was known as 'toupee Tom,' but not to his face, naturally. Bill was a noticeably confident man, middle-aged, with a head of strong white hair and the air of a man who ate fillet steak rather than mince.

Over the next day or two we met several Ethiopians from the government's Department of Mines including two pleasant young geologists who would be joining the scouting trip. Plans were outlined, and a Bell 212 helicopter had been chartered to fly the group first to a town to the north-east called Dire Dawa, where we would meet up with a Russian exploration group. They were conducting a seismic survey in the region under the auspices of a government aid program. The idea was to get some grasp of the logistics of operating in the Ogaden. We would then fly into the area of proposed operations.

We left the hotel in the early morning and drove out to the airport where we met our flight crew, a Canadian pilot and British engineer. The aircraft was painted white with the letters UN printed boldly in black on both sides of the rear fuselage. After some small formalities we boarded the helicopter and took off over the mountains surrounding Addis, flying slightly north of east to Dire Dawa. My only memory of the flight was looking out over the mountainous terrain below and seeing the odd camel that looked so incongruous away from a desert setting.

A support team had been contracted from a South African safari company to supply camping facilities and helicopter fuel once we reached the area of interest. They had already departed so as to be on location when we arrived. We spent the morning checking into a Department of Mines residence that boasted the most beautiful gardens separating the two rows of buildings. They were a cascade of colours from the Bougainvillea and Jacaranda trees. The colours and scents were wonderful.

At lunch we were introduced to the Russian exploration group. The afternoon was quite amusing as the Russian interpreter was very obviously gay, and camp with it. He took an immediate shine to Reggie who was extremely uncomfortable with the situation. They also had an attractive blonde lady whose job title was unclear but there was a definite air of 'entente cordiale' between her and the tall, distinguished leader of the group, who sported a fine moustache.

The afternoon brightened up a little later when we went back to the helicopter and had to wait while the lady attempted to climb aboard wearing a pencil skirt and high heels. The only person who didn't take advantage of her situation was the interpreter who only had eyes for Reggie who, in turn, was doing his best not to get a seat next to him. Anyway, it was gracious of them to show us their operations even if we learned absolutely nothing.

That evening the Russians joined us for dinner, and much Russian vodka was drunk. The more the interpreter drank, so his newfound love for Reggie developed to the point that his boss decided enough was enough and bade us good night taking his crew with him.

We made a reasonably early start in the morning, considering everyone was nursing a hangover from the vodka of the previous night, and were soon heading eastwards out into the prospect. We were all told to keep our eyes peeled for the ground support team, especially as we were by now running low on fuel. Conversation in the helicopter was nigh on impossible except for Reggie and the pilot who had the advantage of speaking through microphones to each other. The rest of us were restricted to cupping our hands and yelling into the ears of the person next to us.

The terrain of the Ogaden was quite different to what we had flown over between Addis and Dire Dawa. It was much similar to what I had imagined Ethiopia to look like from the newsreels of 'Live Aid'. The area was relatively flat and covered with long, dried grass. Bare patches varied between yellow sand and red laterite. There were extraordinarily few signs of habitation. At one point we spotted a small lone army outpost and stopped for a while to check our position from an Ethiopian soldier on duty, and to also ask if he had seen our ground support convoy. He was not at all helpful, so we continued on our way.

Shortly after this stop we spotted a white Toyota Land Cruiser pick-up with two 45 gallon drums in the back. The occupants got out and waved to us, so we prepared to land again, at which point they ran back to their vehicle and sped off along a well-used track. Thinking they were leading us to the main ground support team, we followed them to what turned out to be quite a large village in which we landed.

The moment the pilot switched the engine off we were surrounded by a motley swarm of villagers, and one of them stepped forward and said in good English 'Welcome to Somalia!' This was not what we wanted or expected. It soon became clear that the English speaker was somewhat mentally challenged. In fact he became a potential troublemaker in his wild ramblings saying amongst other things 'Are you from Israel? Are you on a spying mission?' Fortunately, we were the only ones able to understand what he was saying as he moved amongst us. It almost seemed as though he was deliberately taunting us, but he was soon put into the position of mere interpreter once the village headman arrived. For a few moments, though, we were rather worried.

The village headman told us that he had a radio supplied by the government and that he had sent a message to the nearest town and told them of our arrival. This was bad news, and I made my fears known to Reggie who was busily making matters worse by telling all of our party not to mention that we were involved in oil exploration. I told him this was absolutely stupid and a totally unnecessary lie that would trip one of us up in some way or another. He took offence at my unsolicited advice and remained adamant that I should follow his instructions as I was a mere guest.

I next said to Reggie and Bill that I felt this was getting extremely dangerous and as I had five thousand US dollars on me, we should attempt to bribe the headman to turn a blind eye and let us take off back over the border. They both rejected this idea and a couple of hours later the military turned up in two Toyota Land Cruisers complete with mounted machine guns. We were questioned briefly and as dusk fell, we were taken off at great speed. Only the pilot was allowed to remain with the helicopter.

The ride to the army base was pretty scary mainly due to the speed they drove at on poor laterite tracks. Their haste I am sure was due to the fact that once night fell, they would have no control over the area. We arrived miraculously in one piece and were shown into military barrack rooms and given blankets and beds. After a long and arduous day sleep came easy to me.

The next morning, we washed and were given a cooked breakfast consisting mainly of fried kidneys, a local speciality. Most of the Americans declined this on the grounds that offal is not on their list of delicacies. I on the other hand enjoyed them, causing yet another disappointment for Reggie.

A government plane arrived from Mogadishu and we were put on board and flown in relative comfort to Mogadishu's main airport, where we were met by a Somali brigadier who looked a bit like Kenneth Kaunda, the ex-president of Zambia. From the airport we were driven to a larger government-owned detached house in what I took to be an affluent area of the city. We went into the house and were allocated bedrooms. I shared a room with the helicopter engineer, a fellow Brit.

We were given a lecture by the brigadier explaining to us that as we had entered the country illegally, we would be detained there until they decided what to do with us. He then collected our passports from us. At this point we were given the opportunity to shower and change our clothes into the spare set we had carried with us. They fed us a reasonable meal and the brigadier gave us another impromptu talk about nothing in particular, and Reggie asked that our embassies be informed of our presence. This the brigadier promised to do.

Later in the evening the vice-consuls from the American, British and Ethiopian consulates arrived and were introduced to us. They seemed pleasant enough and slightly concerned as to how they were going to get us out of this predicament. However, their assurance that everything would work out fine seemed rather short on detail. We slept well that night, thankful to be in a large 'safe' house.

The next morning after breakfast, the brigadier reappeared and told us everything was going smoothly. He advised us to lie back and enjoy the hospitality of the Somali government. Later that morning the diplomats returned, although the American vice-consul had changed from the previous day. The new one was quite small, young and appeared rather green. He explained that he had taken over the position that very day and his predecessor was returning to the States having completed his tour of duty. The British vice-consul was a very laid-back Welshman who gave the appearance of being somewhat 'passed-over' and had been left to hold the fort in what was obviously a rapidly deteriorating mission. He reminded me a little of Michael Caine in the film adaptation of Graham Greene's novel The Honorary Consul, without the good looks.

Over the next few days we had many meetings, that all ended pretty much the same as the last with no meaningful conclusion. I was able to get them to contact my company's Mogadishu office and the manager, an Australian whom I knew well, was permitted to visit us. He brought us a couple of bottles of Scotch and some paperback novels, all of which were very welcome. We were allowed to walk in the grounds but warned not to approach the gates. They were locked and patrolled by two armed guards.

We were also allowed to go onto the flat roof of the house that was useful for sunbathing during the day, and for Reggie and Bill to plot ridiculous plans of escape that never came to anything.

By now we had been the guests of the Somali government for over a week and still didn't look like being released. Every day the little American diplomat came by and briefed us much the same as the day before. One morning he started the briefing with the classic opening 'Well gentlemen, there is good news and bad news.'

'Give it to us,' we all chorused, 'Bad news first.'

'Well, the bad news is we are no closer to getting you released.'

There was a visible slumping of shoulders. 'And the good news?'

'My wife is pregnant!' he enthused, grinning from ear to ear. I was tempted to ask if he knew who the guilty party was but thought better of it. The silence was deafening.

We spent the days mooching around in groups discussing various options of how we were going to get out of here. People were getting irritable, and Tom's toupee was looking worse by the day. There was never any full agreement that constituted a workable plan. The only person who came close to agreeing with me was Herman, but whenever I said I was going to confront Reggie he always backed out because he basically didn't like the idea of facing his boss.

Finally, one morning about ten days after our capture, the brigadier turned up and smiled as usual, asking how we all were, and in reply dear old Reggie returned the smile and said 'Fine'. This was how it always went.

'   Well, I'm not', I said getting to my feet, 'I'm sorry General' (we always used the American interpretation of the rank of brigadier), 'I can't speak for these gentlemen, but I have work to do in Egypt and if you stamp my passport with an entry visa, I'll get out of your hair.' If looks could kill I would have died the death of a thousand cuts. My intervention seemed to signal an end to the briefing.

Nobody was talking to me at lunchtime. Reggie was sulking and talking in hushed tones to Bill. Then, out of the blue, the brigadier returned in the middle of the afternoon, handed out our passports complete with temporary entry visas and announced we would be leaving on a Kenya Airways flight to Nairobi the next day. I could have kissed him. Everybody thanked him profusely and all we could talk about was leaving, which we did the next morning in a splendid convoy that included the diplomatic vehicles of the three relevant embassies.

Some hours later we were drinking gin and tonics courtesy of Kenyan Airways. On arrival in Nairobi, we checked into a very nice hotel. After going to our rooms everybody headed for the bar where the helicopter mechanic was chatting up several young ladies of the district, and everyone else chatted enthusiastically about our release. My intervention was never mentioned.

The following day we flew back to Addis on a commercial flight and checked back into the Hilton hotel. The plan was to return to Dire Dawa and complete the original mission. I gave my apologies and explained I could not spare any more time and furthermore, I had seen enough of the general terrain to feel confident in making a bid on any seismic contract that might be tendered.

I bade farewell to my hosts that evening and returned to Cairo the next morning. The oil company did tender a contract to all interested geophysical companies and we were successful in winning it.

A Short Space of Time

'Is she with you, Scott?' The morning was not going well for Liz who was frantically searching for her fourteen year old daughter, who had not come home the previous night.

In an attempt to calm her nerves, she had decided to walk the dog, checking places her daughter might be whilst ringing around every phone number she could think of as she went. Scott, her ex-husband, was her last hope.

'Is who with me Liz, and come to that what's it to you; we are divorced now, in case you've forgotten?'

'Debbie our bleedin' daughter.' He just can't help himself, always thinking it was him I was checking up on, she thought, but managed to carry on with her question.

'She didn't come home last night and I'm sick with worry.'

'No, I haven't seen her in weeks; now don't start your usual panicking. Have you checked elsewhere, like her friends for instance?'

'Yes of course I have, and you were my last hope. Have you any idea where she might have spent the night? No, I suppose not, I must get on, I'm trying to walk this stupid dog you left me with. Call me if she gets in touch, won't you?'

'Of course I will, has she got a boyfriend that you know of?'

'I don't think so but then how would I know, I'm only her mother. I think I'll go home, she may be there by now. Bye Scott, sorry to have bothered you.' Making a face at the phone that she wished he could see, she put it in her pocket, pulled the dog around none too kindly and headed for home.

Debbie got out of the car at the end of their street and steadied herself on a lamp post as she waved goodbye to Oscar, who ignored her and accelerated hard away from the kerb the moment she stepped onto the pavement.

Having made it up to their house she was struggling with her door key when she heard her mother call her name from behind.

'Where are on earth have you been Debs?'

'Nowhere much, just with some friends.' She shoved the new iPhone into her pocket and pulled her sleeve down, covering the small puncture bruise on her inner arm.

'What friends? I was worried stiff.' She stopped short from saying that looking at the state of her daughter, she still was.

'Oh come on Mum I wasn't gone long,' she carefully avoided the first half of the question.

'Maybe not, but you know the rules Debbie and the very least you could have done was call me. Come to think of it, perhaps even ask if it was alright to stay out all night.'

'Yeah, okay mum, don't start lecturing me before I even get inside the house will ya, I'm bursting for a pee.'

Once inside, Debbie gingerly climbed the stairs to the bathroom while Liz let the dog into the back garden and filled the kettle to make a cup of tea.

She carried the tea into the living room and flopped down on the settee in a state of complete disappointment bordering on despair. Talking to Scott just now, she realised how she simply wasn't coping on her own.

Sadly, Liz recalled how her own mother said it would only be a short space of time before Debbie went off the rails. Her mum knew of course; she had experienced it with her own daughter.

The White Swan

For Erskine, Tuesdays always seemed to bring even more headaches than Mondays. That took some doing, considering the hangover he suffered yesterday. One day he might learn that bourbon, Bintang beer and Jakarta's climate are a lethal combination.

He was expecting a client in from the field. Harry S. Duimyer was an unknown. The telex said he was an important senior construction engineer on the gas project in central Sumatra.

Shortly after midday Erskine heard the company car pull into the driveway in the office compound. Harry Duimyer was exactly what he had pictured when he read the telex: mid-fifties, heavy-set, tanned with greying hair under a baseball cap emblazoned with the company logo. He wore a white button-down collar cotton shirt, the sleeves rolled half-way up his forearms. In his breast pocket was a passport behind three pens. Halfway down a pair of khaki trousers, the left leg was caught on the top of his light tan work boot, slightly caked with yellow mud.

'Pleased to meet you sir. Come through and have some coffee.' Erskine extended his hand which was firmly shaken. His guest didn't smile. If anything, he looked somewhat sad.

In the office Erskine closed the door behind them. The maid had placed a silver tray with coffee, milk, sugar and a plate of homemade cookies on the teak table in the corner.

'How's it going out there in Sumatra, Harry?' Erskine asked as they sat down.

'As well as can be expected considering this year's monsoons. My guess is that your guys will be a month behind schedule.'

Harry took a sip of his coffee and reached for a cookie. 'Damn fine cookies,' he said, biting a biscuit and regarding the remainder in his hand.

'Thank you, my maid Tina makes them – my wife's recipe.'

'Got your family with you?' Harry asked.

'No. Wife and the boys are back in the States. She didn't like it here – got homesick.'

'Too bad,' Harry sympathised.

For the next hour they talked about the project, then, looking at his watch, Erskine said, 'Heck Harry, you must be starving. The Hotel Indonesia will do us proud. What d'you say?'

'You're in charge, young feller. I could do with some decent chow and a cold beer after that site-canteen garbage.'

As Erskine drove the car out into the mid-week traffic, he tried to gauge his guest. He seemed a nice old boy, looking out at the city without comment, but he hated client entertainment duties, continually walking on eggshells.

'I admire your courage driving in this place, Erskine; I wouldn't have the guts.'

'Been doing it for some time. I have a driver, but when the journey is open-ended and parking's not a problem, I drive myself. I figure if I'm gonna die, it should be my doing and not some local driver.' Erskine gave a wry grin, hoping to get a reaction from his passenger.

Harry said simply, 'Uh-huh,' and continued looking at the passing street scenes.

He parked the car in the shade of a mango tree and they sauntered up the main pathway through the manicured gardens. The huge glass doors were opened by a brightly uniformed doorman who greeted them with a ceremonious bow. To the left of the main reception desk, in the air-conditioned lobby a Gamelan duo played two double rows of round, brass metalliphones, tapping in unison with small mallets, producing a sense of circular rhythm, peace and tranquillity, a marked contrast after the noise of the traffic.

Erskine stopped to allow Harry to watch and listen to the players.

'Ain't that just something else, Erskine?'

Erskine's attention was caught by the approach of a European couple coming towards them from the main foyer. The man was rather nondescript – le Carré's George Smiley perhaps, but the woman was quite stunning. Long, honey-blonde hair resting on tanned shoulders. She was wearing a plain, full-skirted white linen dress.

Gliding through the muted colours of the hotel's Javanese décor she had the appearance of a swan navigating a narrow passage of dark water.

They were twenty feet away when Erskine touched Harry's arm. He seemed mesmerised by the couple. 'Listen Harry I just remembered the restaurant here is not that good on Tuesdays. I know a place that will be much better.' He hurried him back to the car park.

Erskine started the engine when Harry put a hand on his left forearm.

'D'you mind if I ask you a personal question young man?' He was looking closely at Erskine.

'Feel free,' Erskine said.

'You got woman problems?' Erskine nodded. This old boy, hair growing in his ears, probably never been out of Texas before, didn't miss a trick. 'That blonde?' he continued. Erskine nodded again.

'One fine looking lady. Pity she looks spoken for.'

Erskine reversed the car, made a U-turn and drove away.

Tahar's Crossing

Tahar did not feel inclined to go through the emotional drama that would normally be required when a relative undertook a journey of this nature. In his mind his uncle had honoured his duty to his brother, Tahar's father, and he was grateful. All that it was necessary to say had been said many times over. By the same token he was not in the least bit sad to be leaving, even though it was the only home he had ever really known. Deep down he never felt properly part of the family, though the words had never been spoken. He always suspected he was looked upon as a burden to them and their already overstretched family resources.

The morning after the meeting with his cousin, he got up well before the rest of the household to ensure he could use the bathroom and wash himself all over. He changed into clean clothes, putting on the new shirt and jeans bought earlier in the year for this purpose with part of the money he earned picking fruit back in the summer. He pulled his father's old burnoose over the top of this and pushed his head into a new green beanie.

He packed his few possessions, putting the special magazines inside a tee-shirt at the bottom of a small Air Algérie flight bag his cousin in El Oued had given him. He looked around his room one last time and moved into the back of the house and left via the kitchen into the garden. Without stopping, he skirted round the side of the house and out into the street.

Reaching the café, still closed at this early hour, he went around to the back door and knocked before pushing it open. Inside, Fattch the owner was tending to a large oven in the daily process of baking bread and croissants.

He showed no surprise in seeing Tahar and did not stop from his baking beyond giving him a brief nod and a smile. Tahar continued standing and watching the old man work silently away with a begrudging admiration for his talent. It was beyond his understanding how any man could carry on doing the same job day after day, especially as it earned barely a living wage.

Having reached a point where he could break off, Fatteh picked up two croissants in one hand and taking hold of Tahar's elbow with the other, guided him through into the café. Once there he handed the pastries to Tahar and lit the gas burner to prepare coffee. All this in complete silence; it was the actions of two men so familiar with each other that conversation was unnecessary.

After he had prepared two small cups of coffee, thick and sweet in traditional mazboot style, he carried them along with two glasses of water to the table where Tahar was sitting and sat down opposite him.

'So, it is the last I will be seeing you for a while I take it young Tahar, is it? You know I will miss you, but at least my profits might improve a little.' He sipped his coffee, giving Tahar an affectionate smile.

Tahar continued eating the second croissant. He found it difficult to respond without giving way to emotions he was now fighting to control. Next to his cousin, Fatteh represented one of the only people he would genuinely miss once he was gone.

'Yes, today I am going to join my cousin in El Oued. But first I wanted to thank you for all the kindness you have shown me over the years Monsieur Fatteh; I will always think of you.' He used the slurping of his coffee to cover the emotion he was feeling at this moment. As he finished his drink the two men stood up in one movement and hugged one another in a final embrace. As they separated the old man fished into his apron and pulled out several crumpled American twenty-dollar bills and thrust them into Tahar's hand even though Tahar attempted not to accept the money.

'God be with you, go well Tahar; though I am sad to see you go I know it is for the best. There is no future for young people here in Tataouine, or the whole of Tunisia for that matter. I cannot imagine that Algeria is going to be any easier, but you obviously have a plan and that is more than you could manage here. Goodbye and good luck. I want you to have this money. I had been saving it for my son should he have ever got married, but as you know he was killed by those bastards protecting the Binalis' blood-sucking regime. I tried to stop him from going to Sidi Bouzid at the start of the uprising, but he went and paid for it with his life. I have no use for it now.'

With that he turned and went back into his kitchen. There was nothing more to be said, and the atmosphere was thick with emotion mixed with the smell of fresh baking. Tahar shoved the money into his jeans pocket and picked up his bag, unbolted the latch to the front door and let himself out into the street. He searched and found the new imitation Ray Ban sunglasses from the side pocket of his bag and put them on. He had bought them for the journey and though the sun was not yet strong enough for him to need them, they would hide the tears that were starting to form.

Further down the street he stopped at an unmarked taxi stop and waited for the first car heading north. Half an hour later a black Peugeot 504 station wagon pulled up. He was lucky, the car would normally carry anything up to eight passengers but at the moment there was only one. It would take him as far as Gabès. He paid the fare and climbed into a window seat in the back row, thought to be one of the safest seats. Some say that the Peugeot long-distance taxis of North Africa killed more Arabs than the Israeli army.

The taxi pulled away and headed towards the northern edge of town, stopping to pick up two elderly ladies and a young child. Moments later his thoughts wandered to his parents' fatal last trip on this journey. He banished the thought from his mind; it was to be advancement in his life. No time for regrets or sad memories.

On through small settlements they continued, picking up random passengers, and it was not long before the car was full to bursting. Various bags, boxes and containers of all shapes and sizes were tied to the roof-rack causing the car to make exaggerated swaying motions on the many twists and turns of the road. At one point travelling at what could only be described as breakneck speed, the driver was forced to make a dangerous swerve to avoid running down a stray goat. The action caused the passengers to harangue the driver who, turning to argue back, then struck and killed a chicken that had chosen an unfortunate moment to cross the road.

At least no human had lost their life so far. But one old man felt as though part of him had died as he shook his fist at the disappearing taxi and then looked at the dead chicken lying crushed on the tarmac. Having not been dispatched in a proper halal manner it was haram, and only the crows would benefit from this kill.

At Medinine they stopped to allow two passengers to alight and unpack their goods from the roof-rack. Tahar wished he could get out and stretch his legs but being in the back row it was not possible without getting half the load to move. It might also mean he would not get his 'safe' seat back, so he just kept still and quiet. The old man sitting next to him tried to engage him in conversation complaining about the driver and how he had almost killed them swerving to miss the goat. Tahar just politely smiled without commenting. He was not in any mood for meaningless chit-chat. He was glad when the taxi pulled away on the next leg of the journey and he leaned his head against the side window and feigned sleep, in order to deter the old man from any further conversation.

n what seemed but the bat of an eye, the car had stopped again, and the driver was announcing 'Gabès' and Tahar asked the old man to move so that he could get out. It was a little after 10 o'clock in the morning and Gabès was starting to come alive, as it would at this time of the year. A watery sky giving way to a feeble attempt at sun rays offered little respite from the winter chill of the desert, even though they were quite close to the sea.

An old woman assisted by a teenage boy was doing her best to control a small flock of goats and sheep. They looked pathetic and underfed, the goats trying to scavenge on anything and everything that was remotely edible, including odd bits of cardboard and sacking. If it could be moved, it could be chewed.

Tahar pushed through the path of the animals kicking one older nanny-goat who had attempted to chew on his flight bag. The old lady yelled at him not to injure her livestock but then continued to beat the stragglers even harder with a heavy stick. By chance rather than good shepherding, they straggled along in a general but not defined direction. Their intended route was presumably either the market or pastures new. Neither animal nor shepherd was really sure; only the rich had the luxury of forward planning.

A dilapidated ex-army Berliet truck, converted into a passenger bus, made matters even worse by pulling into the square behind the flock and blowing its horn loudly to announce its arrival and therefore potential departure. A teenage boy hung precariously out of the door yelling 'Tozeur, Tozeur' at the top of his voice but anyone further away than 10 metres would never have heard or understood due to the general hubbub and noise of the motor.

The vehicle must have been at least thirty years old and the conversion from truck to bus was not a pretty sight, more like a prop from the movie Mad Max. But Tahar was not deterred from stepping aboard. He wanted to be the first passenger in order to select a seat suitable for the bumpy ride, crossing the bed of the 'Chott El Jérid' and he hoped the causeway was still intact enough to allow them safe passage. Having been an army truck in its former life, it would have originally been equipped with four-wheel drive, essential where they were bound. Whether this still functioned was another matter.

He was well aware that a third-class ride of this nature indicated a fare that would suit his meagre resources. The journey could have been made in much more comfort, courtesy of a new French-made modern coach, possibly equipped with air conditioning. The local bus station was frequented by many such services but would have cost him several times more and in reality, a ride was a ride.

Having selected his seat halfway down the bus he casually watched fellow passengers climb on board for just over an hour. There was no denying he was in good company. Without exception everyone who came aboard was at the lower end of the social scale. Tired and weary peasants whose lives and circumstances managed to keep them just above the gutter. Tahar stood out by being the youngest passenger by far.

As he looked at them one after the other, it reinforced the sense in doing what many had described as foolhardy, leaving his home and country. The gnarled, weather-beaten faces of the old men, the crooked and bent old women, some lugging large sacks of onions just because they cost a few cents less than at their destinations. Not for the first time he wondered what these people had done to deserve a life like this. How could people file into the mosque every Friday and pray to some God who allowed them to live in such misery? He wished he had the answer.

Once the bus was as full as the driver felt it was likely to be, he moved down the aisle taking fares. Every now and again a small argument erupted between him and a passenger either over the amount to be paid or about a complaint over the state of the seats. He only undertook this task because he had never had a bus-boy he could trust to take money. Eventually all fares taken he headed back to his driver's seat and threw the bus into a juddering forward meshing of gears through the cluttered streets. He was using his knowledge of the backstreet labyrinth to avoid the Garde Nationale who would severely impact on his takings and even possibly stop the journey altogether.

For once the journey went without incident after they left the city limits and Tahar settled down to doze once more. He had placed his bag on the outside seat and managed to discourage any fellow passengers from asking him to move it. The bus was not full, so he did not face any serious requests to sit next to him.

In the town of Qibili the bus stopped to take on diesel and water. Tahar draped his burnoose over the seat and carrying his bag left the bus to relieve himself, crouching at the opposite side of the road from the service station. He used the clean sand to wash his hands and then bought a small bag of dates and an orange juice from a makeshift stall next to the fuel pumps before taking up his seat once again. He pierced the small straw into the orange-juice carton and in between sucks slowly ate the dates. The next thing he knew the bus had stopped in a side street in Tozeur and the driver was shaking him.

He wandered through the maze of streets asking the way to the town centre at various shops until he found a small café close to it, so the owner informed him. He ordered a tea and a small pastry. Looking at the clock on the wall as he waited for his order, he noticed it was a little after two in the afternoon. The cloud coverage had broken considerably, and it was pleasantly warm sitting outside at a small rickety table. Inside was the usual assortment of old men, smoking, drinking tea and conversing loudly with one another. He smiled to himself thinking it hardly seemed as though he had left his home – the general scene was identical – just different players.

Paying for his snack he enquired where the long-distance taxis left from and the owner gave him vague directions. His enquiry caused a certain amount of interest from the small group of customers who stopped their discussion for a moment while they turned and looked at the stranger. He had no doubt he would be the topic of their conversation once he was out of earshot.

After a few false starts he found the place where the taxis bound for Hazoua on the border were based. Luckily there was a light green Peugeot 505 station wagon standing almost full. The fact that its front wing was dark blue and stood out from the colour of the rest of the bodywork indicated a previous accident and a standard of taxis that many would prefer not to travel in, and this would reflect in a low priced fare; at least that was the theory. He paid his fare all the way to Hazoua and got in the middle row next to an old couple who were forced to give him a window seat otherwise he might be sitting next to the old lady, and her husband would not tolerate that.

Twenty minutes and two passengers later they were ready to go. They left at a leisurely speed dictated by the condition of the Peugeot more than the intention of the driver. The moment the wheels were turning, he shoved in an old cassette of a collection of well-known songs by an Egyptian female singer and turned up the volume. It was a feeble attempt to compensate for the lack of speed and comfort with entertainment. Most of the other passengers seemed oblivious to the loud singing; for Tahar it was yet another good reason to get as far away as possible from this region. He would not stop until Tunisia was no more than a fading memory.

Rainy Days and Mondays

When I finally got to England, I thought I had died and gone to heaven. After nearly a year of avoiding the police, authorities, traffickers, liars, cheats and so many horrible people in many different countries I had reached my goal physically unharmed. Never mind what it did to my head.

Growing up in a small town in the Sind Province of Pakistan, being a member of the only Christian family in that town had been a miserable life. When my eldest brother Rodney confided in me that he was planning to go to the UK I begged him to take me with him. It took weeks of convincing him to agree, and even then, only after I threatened to tell our mum. I will not dwell on the details of the journey because I prefer to forget about it. The only time I think about it is when I am reminded in my sleep and I wake up in the middle of a nightmare. The night my brother drowned. Leave it at that please.

I would not be telling the truth if I said it was any easier once I finally got to the UK. At least it was safer but life as a refugee in a strange country adds to the scars that you pick up on the way. At least here I had no problem with the language because my father insisted we all learn English from an early age. We went once a week to a Catholic missionary in a nearby town, firstly to pray, and secondly to learn English.

Thankfully that is all in the past. After three hard years of doing all kinds of jobs, most of them illegally, my refugee status came through and I could accept employment legitimately. I was so overjoyed I wrote a long letter to my mum and dad and went to the local post office to send it. While I was waiting in the queue to be served, I began reading the small advertisements on a board. Most of them were for selling items but one was advertising for a cleaner prepared to do laundry. I looked around to make sure no one was paying attention to me. The girl behind me was looking at her phone, so I quickly took the card and stuffed it in the back pocket of my jeans. You learn a lot when you have nothing but your wits.

I ran outside after posting my letter and rang the number on my phone. The lady who answered was very surprised because she said she had only put the card up earlier this morning. She sounded nice but was a little bit suspicious at the speed with which I applied. Then she said she would wait until the next morning to see if there were any other people looking for the job. She said she would call me back. Though I knew nobody else would see the advertisement, I never expected to hear from her. My life as a refugee prepared me for disappointments and broken promises.

But she did, and I got the job. Again, she was more than a little apprehensive when I arrived at her house the following Saturday as requested. What sealed it for me was when she asked me lots of questions, including was I a Muslim, which of course I wasn't. I told her I am a Catholic, and luckily so was she.

The house that I was employed to clean was very nice. Much nicer than any house I had ever entered. I was given a guided tour where the lady explained everything she expected of me as we went. I felt quite scared, but kept it to myself, I hoped. She kept stopping and insisting that she had very high standards of cleanliness, looking at me very intently rather like my mother had done, to make sure I was listening.

Then it came to the question of washing and ironing. My fear went up another level. I had only used a machine in a local laundromat, where the instructions were printed on the wall and there was always someone to ask.

That was six months ago. I'm still in the job. Have I made any mistakes? The honest answer is yes. Funnily enough what saved me was my laundry work. It was my ability to wash and iron her husband's shirts. I don't know what he did when they left the house every day but I do know he needed to be wearing a freshly ironed white shirt. Sometimes two, if they were entertaining.

My brother Rodney used to change his shirt twice a week, and probably only once during the rainy season. This man needed a fresh one every single day no matter what the weather. I have never seen weather like this. Of course, they had an electric drying machine. I hardly ever used it, as nothing compares to a shirt dried naturally, and ironing is so much easier and better.

But today is Monday and the weather forecast on the BBC says showers. I never had to pay any attention to a man or woman telling me about the weather, but I do now, and they are not always right. I dream of those cloudless days back in my village. I imagine my dad's shalwar kameez drying in the sun on the bush outside the front door. I am brought back to reality by remembering the number of times a neighbour would throw dirt on it.

Nobody throws dirt on Mr Hodge's shirts, but having to get them properly dried in this awful weather often gets me down. Especially on Mondays after the freedom of the weekend.

Do Pigeons Ever Get Bored?

'Are you alright Oliver?' Blast, it was the verger's wife Mrs Mutton wandering through the churchyard and there was no lookout to give us the warning – 'Baaaa'.

Gerald Godfrey (or 'Horse' as he was known to his friends) and I were lying in the long grass, poorly maintained thanks to the verger Mr Mutton being off sick with a bad back. We were trying to hit pigeons in the yew trees with marbles fired from my catapult.

'We were watching the pigeons and wondering if they ever get bored, Mrs Mutton.' It was all I could think of in so short a time with no warning. At that moment we were saved, as the first bell started to ring for Morning Prayer.

'You boys really have some daft ideas. But there's the bell; you'd better get yourself into the vestry and get into your cassocks, before the choirmaster is out here looking for you. Go on – do pigeons ever get bored? Whatever next?'

'Phew that was close, Horse.' I whispered as we got up and ran to the back door of the vestry, stuffing my catapult into my blazer pocket as we went.

Inside the vestry the creep Melvin Walton was pulling the bell rope making it look like it was some form of a dark art, when in fact anybody could do it. I even did it one Evensong when I happened to be the first there to volunteer and Walton was away. Fifteen minutes later and we were all attired in cassocks, surplices and ruffs, and positioning ourselves in two lines behind the creep Walton who not only claimed the position of bell-ringer, but also the carrier of the staff and brass cross leading us two by two up the aisle.

This was the part I liked most as we silently walked between the assembled parishioners, trying our best to look meek and mild while sneaking looks towards the nearest pews to see if there were any new girls present. Horse and I walked behind the creep with me on the left, in order to peel off and get the nearest seat on the left-hand choir stall and the best view of the congregation.

Our choirmaster and organist, crabby Crabbe, was bashing away on the organ using the mirror set up to give him a view of us filing into place so he could see when to stop his opening piece. His playing was quite funny as he pushed and pulled various stops, pressing the keyboard in a very dramatic way, his head moving in time with the music. This opening piece was his pride and joy and he attacked it with gusto. It was the only time he ever appeared to be really happy.

Once the last of the grown-up singers were in position behind us trebles and the creep had secured the staff and cross, making a big deal over his genuflection as though he was Gregory Peck or something, we prepared to lower the hinged choir stall seat into position. That was when my plan to ogle the blonde girl in the front pew went horribly wrong. You see, the bench seat us seven choirboys were sitting on rested on three wooden brackets and I was sitting over one of the end ones, and my longest finger got trapped between the seat and the bracket.

How I managed not to scream out I will never know. Trying to explain in sign language to six idiot choirboys to get up enough for me to get my finger out from under the seat took forever. Close to fainting, I left the stall, quickly crossed myself and shot out of the other side door next to old Crabbe, who was glaring at me with that look I knew so well from rehearsals.

Once out in the open churchyard I was able to let out a huge yell and burst into tears. My right hand, long finger was white, twice its normal width and hurting like I have ever felt in my life. My yell must have alerted Mrs Mutton who came shuffling round the corner with a sickle in her hand. Scared and frightened as I was, I thought she was going to attack me, and I cowered away from her.

'What on earth are you yelling about Oliver, and why are you out here?' I couldn't speak; words wouldn't come out. I continued crying and held my hand up to show her my injured finger. 'Well boy, that be God's retribution for attacking his innocent birds and telling lies. That's what that be.'

Hotel Berinichi

Ali and his young brother, Omar, were busy playing with a large scorpion they had found under a rock. They were teasing it with a Zippo cigarette lighter. It was their only possession they had left belonging to their father, who had disappeared during the last days of Gaddafi's rule.

They were engrossed in the game when a low flying, black and green, small aircraft shot over their heads before they were even aware of its approach. The noise and the backdraft caused them both to duck involuntarily and curse in unison. The sheep they were tending also let out a cacophony of frightened bleats and scattered in all directions. The brothers looked at one another in a combination of bewilderment, then horror as they realised the scorpion had escaped.

On board the unregistered Twin Otter the only passenger was Terry Narang, an Anglo-Pakistani, who sat in the co-pilot's seat in a mixture of terror and admiration at the pilot's skill flying at what seemed only inches above the rocky jebel below them.

They had flown for just under an hour after crossing the Mediterranean coastline and now the rocky landscape started to give way to undulating sand and occasional rock and rough scrub. Ten minutes later the pilot punched Terry's shoulder, pointed through the right hand windscreen and yelled, 'There she blows.'

As they got closer he could make out a crude landing strip marked with two lines of blackened 45 gallon oil drums. Moments later they were safely on the ground. The landing was much smoother than he had anticipated. It took only a few minutes for Terry and the pilot to lift his motorbike and backpack off the aircraft and shake hands. The pilot taxied back down the strip, did a quick U-turn and took off halfway along it.

Two hours later, having negotiated the track along the pipeline, he was speeding along the main blacktop between Derna and Benghazi.

As planned, this being Ramadan, dusk was the ideal time to enter the city as the inhabitants were about to partake of Iftar, the breaking of the fast. As he progressed through the outer suburbs of Benghazi proper, he heard the recorded sound of a cannon firing, the official sign for the frantic rush for nicotine, caffeine and food to commence.

The city was a complete mixture of new developments pushed on top of and in between the old, crudely and with little thought. However, the new buildings hadn't lasted long due to many having been destroyed in the recent battles of Libya's chapter of the Arab Spring.

The Berinichi Hotel, though part of earlier times, miraculously survived both development and war. At this moment it was only of interest to one lone motorcyclist closing in on it by pre-set coordinates on satellite navigation. Entering the hotel grounds, he switched off his headlight and coasted as quietly as possible around to the back of the main building. The moment he stopped and climbed off the motorcycle a tall figure dressed in a brown camel-hair burnoose stepped out of the shadow of the building and approached him.

'Salaam alaykum,' he spoke softly yet clearly and bowed imperceptibly, placing his right hand across his heart as he did so.

'Alaykum salaam,' Terry returned the greeting.

'You have made good time Narang, or would you prefer I call you Terry?' His voice was very deep and his Arabic was genteel, well spoken. His question went unanswered. 'Follow me.' With that he turned and walked towards a small outhouse at the back of the main building. Opening a battered wooden door he ushered Terry to move inside with the motorcycle. Once inside he closed the door and switched on the light, a single unshaded bulb hanging from the ceiling. Terry pulled the machine up on its stand and silently followed his new associate's example in covering the machine with various bits of old tarpaulin, concealing its shape completely.

The Arab motioned him outside and switched off the light, closing the door behind them and locking it. They passed along the back of the hotel and entered a small metal door at the far side of the building. It contained nothing other than a wooden bed with a filthy stained mattress, a small table and chair and was lit by a fluorescent lamp. On the table were an open cardboard box of bottled water and a bag of fresh dates. Numerous cobwebs stretched across the ceiling and walls.

'Wait here for a while, eat and drink,' Before he could make any reply the Arab disappeared out of the door. It was done in such a way, with such stealth and the rapid opening and closing of the door, it was as though he hadn't ever been in the room.

He pulled his backpack off, threw it onto the bed and sat down on the chair, opened one of the bottles of water and took a long swig followed by a handful of dates. Minutes later the door opened and a much shorter man entered, wearing a dark blue tracksuit. Terry started to get up, but the man gestured for him to remain seated with several motions of his outstretched crippled hand. The newcomer was, he guessed, in his late twenties but gave the appearance of someone who had experienced many hardships in his short life. He was slightly stooped and underneath his sparse beard there was a prominent crescent-shaped scar running from his earlobe to the corner of his mouth. He wore a cheap pair of sunglasses despite the hour. On his feet was a pair of scuffed black leather shoes with the backs trodden down.

He spoke quietly in rasping Arabic that Terry had difficulty in understanding. 'Ready?' It was plainly rhetorical so Terry nodded, though he would have liked to have finished the dates. 'You will not be given or make any written instructions at any point. Ever! Understood?' Again, Terry simply nodded but openly showed his irritation at such unnecessary remarks. He could sense in turn the man's dislike of such open hostility.

The man fished into his tracksuit pocket and came out with a grubby mobile phone and charger which he handed to Terry. 'There are many numbers in the memory. Genuine numbers but only the last one, Zsa Zsa, will know who you are. She will answer as your fiancée, she is in Tunis. Is that clear? Only the last one; now give me your own phone.' He again emphasised his words as though anticipating resistance. Terry maintained his stare and nodded without reply. He wished he could see his eyes. He knew this was coming but it still unnerved him, severing the last slender thread of contact with the world outside. He felt a distinct cold feeling of melancholy passing through him as he handed it over.

The final commitment, he was totally at their mercy now. To counteract this awful feeling and occupy his mind he flipped open the new phone, looked first to see it was fully charged and then scrolled down to the last name and snapped it shut.

'Now I will take you to your room. You are in room 24. You will never be visited at that room, understood? If you are, it will be either a mistake or your enemy. Wash and sleep fully clothed. You will be contacted by three rings on the hotel phone. When you receive those rings take your belongings, leave the door open and go to the main entrance. A Toyota station wagon will be waiting for you. Get into the car without speaking to anyone including the driver. He is deaf and dumb so questions will be pointless. Do you have any questions for me?'

'No none, you have made it easy to understand,' Terry lied unconvincingly.

'Good. Follow me and avoid looking at anybody on the way. You can be certain there is no-one of interest staying here.' Terry stood, put the phone and charger into his knapsack and fell in behind the man. He was not difficult to follow as he walked very slowly, dragging his right foot as he went. They made a strange pair indeed.

When they reached the room the man unlocked the door and gave Terry the key. Without another word he turned and left him to enter. Terry pushed the door open; the light was already on. After a quick look around he entered, closed the door and locked it, leaving the key in the door. The room was about as basic as he had ever seen before. He had been billeted in better accommodation on active duty.

He stripped, washed, dressed quickly and lay down on the single bed. The bed linen was of a quality that would have had him remain fully clothed even if he had not been instructed to do so. He tossed the grubby pillow onto the floor and used his knapsack instead. He left the light on and, surprisingly, fell instantly asleep, only waking briefly around two o'clock to use the toilet. From that point on he only slept fitfully and was relieved when the phone gave three loud rings just after five o'clock.

Following his instructions to the letter he went out into foyer. The marble floor was filthy and water-stained; what furniture there was looked so rickety it would defy any use. He skirted the broken pieces and made for the main door. There was no one around as he passed through the cracked glass doors and climbed into the Toyota that was sitting outside with the engine running. The moment he closed the passenger door the driver pulled away. A scant look around the cab revealed nothing particularly unusual other than the absence of seatbelts.

They drove for just under an hour, westwards, away from the hotel before turning north along a rough unmade road comprised mainly of soft sand. Cresting a small hill, he could see a medium-sized, white stucco house surrounded by a ten-foot-high wall. On the east side of the grounds a clump of scraggy palm trees swayed in the dawn breeze. A hundred metres or so beyond was the shoreline; the sea was quite calm and no-one was in sight. When they were within twenty metres of a pair of faded blue gates they opened automatically and then closed behind them once they were inside.

As he climbed out of the Toyota he saw the tall figure who first met him the previous day standing there watching him. He had changed out of his burnoose and was wearing a pristine white gallabiyah. 'Good morning Narang, I trust your night at the Berinichi was comfortable?' He smiled, extended his hand and spoke in almost perfect English in the unmistakable way of well-educated North African Arabs. His manner was serious but friendly.

'Morning? Why all this crap, couldn't we have dispensed with all this bloody subterfuge and been at this point last bloody night?' Relief and anger combined to cause a flood of discontent to spill out of him.

'Surely you of all people can understand. The time between our meeting last night and this minute were the most dangerous since you climbed aboard your aircraft in Cyprus. You could say it was the only way I could test the security, and if it had failed you might not be alive. I once flew from London to my home in Cairo and the British Airways pilot announced that now we had landed we faced the most dangerous section of our journey, from the airport to our hotels. Your journey was similar but more dangerous.'

The difference between the interior and exterior of the house was literally that of night and day. Inside, the windows were all firmly shuttered and consequently all the lighting was artificial.

'Help yourself to coffee and pastries,' the Arab gestured towards an ornate low table assembled by means of a large brass circular tray mounted on an intricate carved wooden stand. Seated cross-legged on one of several leather pouffes, Terry took a sip of coffee; it was thick and scented with cardamom. He followed this by demolishing three of the small pastries while his host simply watched him in silence.

Having given him sufficient time to eat several more pastries and drink two more cups of coffee, the Arab went to a large, lacquered dining table and bade Terry to join him. On the table was a big black and white map held down on each corner by a smooth pebble. The map intrigued Terry as he had never seen such a large scale detailed one of Tripoli before. There were several markings in red felt tip pen indicating points of interest mainly close to the coast, which was obviously the main harbour.

'Where on earth did you get this from?' His question was ignored. Instead, the Arab pointed to one compound containing six identical buildings.

'In here beats the heart of Tripolitania's strategy to transport thousands of Muslim immigrants to Western Europe quickly and efficiently, unlike the amateur efforts of private schemes currently leaving these shores to Italy.' He watched Terry carefully as the information sank in.

'Your task is not one that many men would take dispassionately. You have to be on the first boat scheduled shortly, and make sure that it goes to the bottom of the sea.'

'Before or after it has its cargo is on board?'

'After, and once it has left the harbour.' The reply came as a complete shock and Terry was forced to use all his concentration not to show his true reaction.

'Let me get this straight. You want me to scuttle a passenger ship full of people – is that correct?'

'Not exactly; it is a cargo vessel that will be illegally concealing a couple of thousand potential immigrants. It is a grand scheme to import a lot of people to an already overlarge population of North Africans in southern France particularly around Marseilles. It is essential that we cause this scheme to fail and, fail spectacularly.'

'Oh it will be spectacular alright. What on earth do you expect to achieve by this?'

'Come on Narang can't you see? Why, there are so many pluses here. First the stupid Europeans, in particular the French with that myopic little man, and the Germans with that ugly Hausfrau will start to see what is really happening. Secondly those brainless idiots in Tripoli will have engendered so much hatred it will bring them down and the infighting will reach such a level that NATO intervention will be all but welcomed. But most importantly, the ridiculous current levels of migration will stop instantly and, it is calculated, with a little more encouragement will start to reverse. Don't you see this will rival 9/11?'

'I can see that alright, the big difference is I am not a bloody suicide bomber, am I? I will have the death of all those people on my hands, forever!' He allowed his horror to show.

'Stop being such a, how do you say, drama queen. Can you imagine how the pilots who dropped atom bombs on Japan felt? How many of your squadron or regiment have taken on jobs that were repugnant to their better nature? Once upon a time we could rely on America to carry out unpopular actions but ever since they elected that African into the White House their balls have dropped off. As for the next in line, that disgusting wife of Clinton, she couldn't even save her own ambassador right here in Benghazi, could she?'

'I should feel honoured that you compare me to such brave men, but I don't. When we stand here casually talking about what I am expected to do it comes to mind that I am a major in the British

Army you know. My training was based on killing opposing combatants not civilians. I have killed people before, but you must realise I've never contemplated anything like this.'

'Look Major, this is not the time or the place for this conversation. A lot of planning and international co-operation has brought us thus far. You did come highly recommended and I never expected this kind of reaction.'

'I'm sorry, there is no need to talk like that. On every assignment I've undertaken I have had moments of doubt and in some cases regret; it's just that it would have been nice if some chicken-shit politician in London had taken the time to spell out exactly what the target was. It takes a little bit of getting used to. I might have what is required for such an operation, but I have also got a heart not a fucking swinging brick, you know. When I agreed to take this on I thought I would be plotting against Isis, not hundreds of civilians no matter how much we don't want them. First things first; please let you and I get down to some basics, like what is your name?'

In the scrub behind their house, Ali and Omar had found a deadly fat-tailed scorpion. Ali knew they should leave it, but Omar insisted on getting out their father's Zippo. He liked dangerous games.

And Pigs Did Fly

'Is he my real dad?' Henry looked up at his mother, visibly shaken after the most recent fight with the man in question. He had just left, slamming the door so hard it was a miracle it was still on its hinges.

His mother Jocelyn stopped momentarily from picking up a chair that had been knocked over in the fracas to wipe the blood that was trickling down her chin from a cut on her lip. 'That truly is a good question son. I 'spose you are of his blood (in truth she wasn't absolutely sure), but if you want to call him dada, that's up to you.' She moved over to the sink, wetted a tea towel under the cold water tap and dabbed cautiously at her cut lip.

'Well, is there anyone else I can choose?' At ten years old and never living with anyone other than his mother all of his life, the question was beyond him. On the one hand Henry didn't want to choose the man who periodically burst in on their lives creating mayhem, but conversely, somewhere in his undeveloped sense of male loyalty, it seemed wrong to deny him as his father if in fact he was.

As if to delay answering the question he carried on where his mother left off, picking up bits and pieces that lay strewn around the floor.

Jocelyn's thoughts turned to more immediate problems of what to feed the boy with before she went on her night shift at the care home. 'I'll make you a fried egg sandwich for your tea. You like them, don't you?' The boy had not eaten since his school dinner at midday but looking in the fridge she knew there was little choice.

'Yes, that's okay and anyway I ain't that hungry 'cos I got Abbie's piece of pizza at school. I dunno why her mum puts her in for school dinners 'cos she only ever eats the puds, and not always them.'

'That's 'cos they's free boy, that's why. If she be payin' herself she wouldn't, believe me.' She finished tending her lip and set about making his sandwich.

Looking up from the egg sizzling in the frying pan she glanced over at her son. 'What you goin' to be doin' tonight boy? Did they give you any homework?'

'No, I was thinking of going along to see Abbie, but she said her dad was visiting so I might just watch TV for a while, I fink there's a football match on later.' He shoved his hands deep into his pockets and shrugged his shoulders. He did his best to smile even though he was still concerned over the father subject.

'Ain't you got no boys to play wiv?'

'Yeah, but the uvver side of Peckham so we only get the chance at school or sometimes at the weekend. I'm alright mum, really.' He wasn't, and the truth was he was scared to leave the flat by himself at night. He'd been threatened more than once for not being a member of any of the gangs.

She finished the sandwich and put it down on the table for him along with their last can of Coca-Cola. 'There you are, I knows it ain't much, but it should see you right till I gets paid tomorrow and we can have a real meal. Now, Leroy said he was coming back later so you'd better keep the door locked. Is that understood? Lock it and bolt it after I leave for work, you hear me now?'

'Yeah momma okay I will.' He carried his plate and can to the sink and went into the other room, flopped onto the sofa and switched on the television and started to channel-hop settling on *The Simpsons* halfway through an episode.

His mother came into the room dressed in her care home blue and white uniform. She had managed to hide some of the cut on her lip with make-up. 'I'm off now Henry, remember what I said about locking the door now. I'll see you in the morning before you head off, bye. Oh, I nearly forgot if you get into any problem you call Mrs Ayalougu in number 32. I never thought that we would ever need the help of some Hausa, us bein' Christian an' all but she's been good to us and she knows how to deal with the likes of Leroy.' With that she left.

Henry woke with a start; Leroy had cuffed him around the head. He had fallen asleep during the football game and had no idea what time it was. Startled and scared he realised he had forgotten to lock the door.

'Where is she? Come on look lively you little shit, where is that bitch? I won't ask you agin before you get the choice of 'ospital or the morgue.' He thrust his tattooed fists one after the other at the boy who was attempting to shrink away from him to the far end of the sofa.

Leroy, unsteady and the worse for drink, leaned over and grabbed the boy, catching hold of him around his slender upper arm. Henry instinctively bent his head and sunk his teeth into Leroy's index finger and bit with all his might.

'Yeow, you little shit you're gonna regret that.' He snatched his hand away and Henry shot around the room away from him into the kitchen and out of the main door on to the balcony.

His first thought was to go to number 32 as his mother instructed, but something changed his mind. He knew if he ran, he would possibly escape this once, but it would not be permanent. A red mist took over his fear as he braced himself against the balcony wall and faced the vision of Leroy lunging out of the door at him. Instinctively he dropped to his knees, grabbing hold of the big man's right thigh with both his arms. The combination of Leroy's mad rush and missing his prey threw Leroy completely off balance. Henry heaved himself upright with all his strength, sending his assailant clean over the balcony. With a blood curdling scream Leroy sailed head first into thin air landing with a loud crash onto the rubbish containers three levels below.

Everything went eerily silent for several moments. Henry sat on the floor, his legs now outstretched in front of him, his face devoid of any expression apart from the mildest look of self-satisfaction. Job well done. Several doors opened and residents ran to look over the balcony first to where Leroy's body lay in an ungainly repose over the bins, then to Henry.

Amongst the gasps and chatter Henry heard the calming voice of Mrs Ayalougu from 32 who was patting his arm and helping him to get up. She was smiling a huge grin on her broad face showing the big gap where her front teeth used to be. 'It be alright now young Henry. You go on back inside and I'll call the law. You and me will have a little talk before they get here, okay? We'se goin' to tell them that pigs can fly ain't we?'

The Return of the Native

Alex had returned from a lifetime in Africa where he'd been content and treated as a celebrity by virtue of the colour of his skin and his position in the bank. That was before it became nationalised. It happened rather suddenly and, as he had always kept a flat in his home town, he simply returned there. It wasn't planned; the bank arranged the shipping of his belongings; it was the only address he could offer them. Most of it ended up in the charity shops as it was either too big or unsuitable for the flat.

The weather, his fellow members at the city sports club and his leisure time, he could only dream about now. Then there was the lovely Joyce, who joined him most weekends and never took anything for granted, or as she put it so eloquently in local philosophical terms, 'no condition is permanent.' Alex gave her money and clothes; Joyce gave him pleasure and honesty. Love was a possible feature of the relationship, but if it was it was never mentioned. He was, by and large, a man for whom married life offered no attraction whatsoever and he saw no reason or purpose in changing his status.

They met when she was working in a department store; she was only seventeen at the time, and for the first and only time in his life Alex was smitten. They were together for nearly twenty years until she was accidentally killed crossing the road one morning on her way to work. Alex suffered her loss in absolute private silence. He never mentioned her death to any of his colleagues and he never met any of her family. Naturally everyone on both sides knew of the relationship but he never publicly acknowledged the liaison.

To grieve in this way had a profound effect on him and he became even more insular. It was as though Joyce and he had never met. His maid once tried to offer her condolences but was told in no uncertain terms that if she valued her job, never to mention the subject again. She in turn quickly advised his driver to act accordingly.

He never talked about his life in Africa when he resettled in England, and certainly not to his only living relative, his sister. He could only imagine her shock and horror if he had done so. She in turn secretly assumed he was gay.

That was in another life. Now, as he observed his fellow citizens at moments like this, he wondered why he had bothered to return to this, his homeland. But then where else to go? Not for the first time he began to realise that he was just as much a stranger here as he was in Africa. The long period of his life as an expatriate had somehow denuded him of a true identity. There he was a different colour; here he was simply different.

His thoughts meandered, as they did at moments like this: Friday lunchtime when he was coerced into agreeing to meet his sister for lunch. She was late as usual. Fortunately, this assignation didn't happen too often, as after half an hour she would accept they didn't really have anything in common other than blood. He on the other hand often thought the milkman might have got in there somehow. They were so different, and his inability to offer anything meaningful in conversations she found irritating. But at least in her mind it gave her company, which occasions were few these days since she lost her husband Frank. It was also the only chance she got to relieve her mean and boring brother of some of his ill-gotten gains by way of a free meal.

It also meant it was Alex who now had the onerous task of substituting for her late husband by listening to her litany of minor aches and pains that the local NHS was in her opinion incapable of treating properly. He recalled with a wry smile one of the last times he visited Frank in the general hospital not long before he died. Though she was there to visit her dying husband she used the opportunity to recount a list of her own ailments. Frank had looked fed up and whispered to him that 'he wished her tongue was as tired as his ears.' She chose to ignore him as she had throughout their married life.

Scanning around the restaurant he started to pay attention to his fellow diners. At one of the centre aisle tables sat two elderly ladies, slowly and deliberately tucking into their meal. Their table was surrounded by various walking aids; a blue four-wheeled contraption with handlebars, brakes and a small satchel-bag for one, and a pair of walking sticks hooked precariously over the back of a chair for the other. There was very little conversation between them as they slowly ate their meal looking around at other tables from time to time. There was a certain fox-like appearance to their actions as if they were devouring stolen fare. Alex smiled at one of them when she looked in his direction but either she didn't notice or chose to ignore him.

At another table sat two well dressed women, mother and daughter he assumed, with a young baby in a high chair to one side. The child seemed happy and well-fed; its podgy cheeks gave the impression of a kookaburra chick seeking a feed from a mother hen as it took intermittent sucks on a proffered feeding bottle. After a few noisy gulps, it happily pushed the bottle away and attempted a small handclapping exercise that resulted in a rattle being knocked to the ground. The mother bent and retrieved it as though embarking on the start of a game for the child's benefit.

He looked over to his left at the next table beyond the elderly ladies who, having finished their main course were deep in discussion, presumably about the choice of desserts. At the next table were a middle-aged couple sitting without talking, in that air of boredom that surrounds two people who have expended all points of conversation after years of being in each other's company. They were conspicuously too well dressed for such a time and place; the small feathery fascinator on the lady suggested they were about to attend a wedding or some such occasion and needed to kill some time. Suddenly the lady started talking, and the man looked around as though he thought she was talking to someone else and sought to identify who it might be, before realising that she was addressing him.

One table down from them sat another couple acting out a familiar scene. They were casually dressed in clothes suited to someone half their age and well beyond their sporting prowess; the waitress was just serving their order. The man was given a simple sandwich while the lady was served with what appeared to be a multi-layered hamburger, large enough to challenge the jaws of a boa constrictor, accompanied by a miniature tin bucket of chips. They both had a bottle of imported lager which they sipped without the aid of a drinking glass.

Having delivered the food, the waitress approached Alex's table on her way back to the counter and stopped to say that his wife had just arrived, indicating with her eyes and turn of her head, the entrance by the counter. He looked for a split second as if in a dream, thinking he would see the ebony features of Joyce but no, his eyes delivered the true vision; a tall thin woman dressed in mauve was waving to him.

'Oh, that's just my sister' he sighed, 'thankfully, not my wife, it's that time again.' He waved in her direction and forced the briefest of smiles. The waitress, herself a single-parent immigrant and streetwise, grasped that the remark required no reply, left the words in the air and continued her way back to the counter thinking to herself, 'I'll never understand these British'.

The Mayor's Card

The morning that Stephie George's half-naked body was discovered in Swindon's goods yard by a railway policeman's German Shepherd caused a series of surprises all around the town as the news spread along the gossip channels.

First the policeman recognised her as the singer who often performed at the Hornets' Nest night club. He remembered vividly her husky voice and particularly her rendition of 'Blue Velvet'.

The next person to be shocked was Detective Sergeant Tony Harris who attended the murder scene. He recognised her straightaway as the woman who had served him in the Tesco Express the previous day. He had never attended a crime scene where the victim was known to him, a coincidence that he felt uncomfortable with.

But the biggest surprise of all came on the slab in the mortuary when it was found that Miss Stephie George was in fact Mr Stephen George, a thirty-five-year-old man. The number of Swindon males who had admired Stephie's cleavage over the years ran into considerable numbers. The shame and self-loathing would spread through the town like a plague, and for some more than for merely lusting.

However, the biggest shock and embarrassment would be felt in the town mayor's office when the police pathologist discovered the mayor's crumpled, damp business card in Stephie's hand.

Recently elected after unfounded allegations regarding business associations with the underworld failed to block his appointment, Mayor Reginald George was about to face his biggest challenge.

A Hard Rain's Gonna Fall

Hassan Nawaz glanced at his wife Kadisha fast asleep on the far side of the bed to ensure she had not sensed his getting up. He knew that if she was aware of his departure before dawn it would only cause her to fret, and that would awake the children and not only delay him but increase his own nervousness.

Picking up his clothes carefully and silently from the floor he carried them into the kitchen where he quickly dressed. Opening the back door, he retrieved his work boots, closed the door and tiptoed barefoot out to his pickup. Leaning against it for support he pulled the boots on over his bare feet. Reaching up under the eaves of the house he pulled out a long, narrow canvas bag and laid it in the back of the pickup.

He opened the door of the pickup and slipped into the driving seat, inserted the ignition key, switched to the on position and held the door closed without slamming it shut. The pickup was parked facing down the gravel slope outside the house to allow him to bump start the vehicle in case the battery was flat or the engine too cold to turn over with the starter motor. Slipping the handbrake off while simultaneously dipping the clutch the pickup rolled silently down onto the track below their house where he lifted his foot from the clutch, the engine spluttered into life and he drove down the track towards the main road. Once there he turned south, towards Wadi Natrun in the direction of Cairo.

In the meeting the previous night at the house of the local Imam it had been decided that he, Hassan, the senior and most experienced member of this local band, would carry out this assignment.

The Mobil service station at the turn off to Wadi Natrun was bathed in yellow electric floodlights giving it an eerie, haunted appearance. A couple of mangy dogs broke the silence making feeble, half-hearted barks but seeing he was simply turning up the dirt road alongside the station they flopped back down, not bothering to give chase. The night watchman sound asleep in the office never registered the passing vehicle.

He drove for twenty minutes or so just on sidelights. It was quite misty as was often the case at this time of year and main beam would only intensify the fog; besides he knew there was little or no danger of any traffic coming the other way.

Traversing the road around the next curve, the Coptic monastery lights suddenly came into view. His information was that senior clergy would be leaving to go to Cairo at first light. He turned the pickup onto the road to the right and started to climb a not inconsiderable hill; the front drive wheels found it difficult to keep traction causing the light pickup to bounce over the rough, uneven surface. It only took a few minutes before he reached the top of the hill and swung around to face the direction of the monastery and switched off the lights and the engine.

Now in complete silence he could see streaks of sunlight starting to filter over the irregular horizon away to the east. He opened the pickup door and stepped down from the cab, reaching for the canvas bag in the back; he untied the two lengths of rope from around it and pulled out a hunting rifle, complete with telescopic sights.

After making a thorough check of the firearm, he leaned over the left hand side of the bonnet and adopted a firing position directed at the monastery. Looking through the telescopic sights he adjusted the focus onto the centre of the building and the tall double main doors. Illuminated by a single overhead lamp, he could see clearly the bolts on the large brass door hinges.

He laid the rifle carefully on the bonnet of the pickup and moving back to the door felt inside the cab for the large bottle of water wrapped in a small prayer-mat that his wife had placed under the seat, as she had done every evening since they were married. He removed his boots, and using the water from the bottle, set about the ritual cleansing required before prayer. He then turned to face the direction of the splinters of sun on the far horizon and began his daily prayers.

He'd never missed a day since his father's execution. He had been hanged by the military junta along with nine others convicted of an attack on the Cathedral in Zamalek during the Arab Spring. His only crime was being an old friend of the late father of one of the attackers. Hassan made a special request in the prayer to carry his bullet straight, to avenge his father's death.

Finishing his prayers, he replaced the water bottle back inside the cab, returned to the front of the truck and picked up the rifle again.

If his information was correct, in ten minutes the Coptic Bishop would come through those doors. Hassan had never killed another human being before and he pondered momentarily how it would feel, before dismissing the thought from his mind.

There was comfort in recalling the Imam's words, 'the executioner's face is always well hidden.'*

*Remembering Bob Dylan – 'A Hard Rain's Gonna Fall'

Sunday – The Sound of Silence

The Reverend Paul Burroughs looked around the dining room of the hotel and beyond his fellow guests to the River Avon, and the cathedral across the meadows where he had been summoned later that afternoon.

He finished his coffee and drained the last drop from his wine glass, willing the alcohol to bring him the strength to accept whatever decision the Bishop was about to deliver. He signed the bill the pretty young blonde waitress had left at his side and returned to his room.

Sitting on the edge of his bed he attempted without success to read a passage from his bible, the copy his mother gave him the day he was ordained almost twenty years ago to this day. But the thoughts of recent events in his parish kept flooding back into his mind and made reading impossible.

He carefully closed the bible, placed it back on the bedside table, stood up and walked towards the window. Once again he looked at the cathedral spire and then at the river, now swollen by the early autumnal heavy rains the previous week. The current was fast moving and carrying several bits and pieces of fallen branches.

It would be so easy to circumvent what he knew in his heart of hearts would be the outcome of his meeting with the Bishop by the simple act of quietly slipping into that river unnoticed.

But suicide was never in his DNA, so kicking off his shoes he picked up the remote and switching on the television to the first channel, stretched out on the bed only to nod off moments later. During the sleep he had a series of strange dreams, culminating in a nightmare scene where he had been condemned to die, placed in position like one of the founding bishops lying in the cathedral, and told to remain there until he stopped breathing.

The scene caused him to awaken, sweating and alarmed. Looking around the room to gather his whereabouts he was surprised to notice that his travel clock showed he had been asleep for almost two hours. He went to the bathroom, cleaned his teeth, combed his hair and prepared to meet his fate.

Minutes later he was climbing the elevated section of pavement at the end of the street as it curled round and rose to the bridge over the river downstream from the hotel. As he came in full view of the bridge itself, he noticed a young girl dressed in a red hoodie, blue jeans and strangely, barefoot.

The figure in the red top looked as if she was trying to climb onto the wall, then stopped when she saw him coming. He continued walking towards her, rehearsing in his mind how to approach the subject that looked as though she was preparing to jump. But his concern was unnecessary for he never got beyond saying 'Excuse me.'

The girl whirled around to face him, her face contorted in a white rage as she slapped him hard around his face with such force that his spectacles flew off over the bridge wall into the river below and he fell against the wall, painfully grazing the left side of his face on the rough stonework.

It was over in a flash; the girl fled the scene leaving him sitting there dazed, until moments later he unlaced his shoes, removed them, stood up and silently launched himself over the parapet into the river.

His body was discovered half a mile downstream, caught up on a large branch. A lady nearby had been alerted by the sound of a dog howling, which was found desperately clinging to the branch. It transpired the dog had been reported missing by a guest at the hotel earlier that afternoon.

The vicar's elderly mother was quoted as saying that her son must have dived in to save the dog, as he was passionate about animal welfare. A week later Wiltshire constabulary said they were not treating the death as suspicious.

The unpaid hotel bill was settled by the Bishop's secretary who said that he had been expected for tea with the Bishop that afternoon and they had been concerned when he didn't arrive. The next day a Polish chambermaid left her employment with the hotel unexpectedly, returned home to her native town of Gdansk and applied to enter a convent.

Three weeks later a funeral service was held in the village of the Reverend Burroughs' adopted home. The service was officiated by the Bishop and it was widely reported on the local news. The local RSPCA inspector read the eulogy. A thirteen-year-old Iranian immigrant choirboy fainted during the service. His adoptive mother said he was very upset because it brought back memories of his journey to Europe, and he had been very attached to the vicar who was helping him with his plans to become a professional football player

Journey Into Space

The daily walk down the hill allows one time to reflect on the forthcoming journey and the hope of a successful conclusion. Enter the 'Halls of Healing' taking care to avoid the grand prix of heavy-duty wheelchairs travelling to and fro, pushed by porters or friends.

A choice of elevators or stairs; no brainer – stairs – get those 'bungalow knees' in action. Down two levels to the radioactive vaults, follow the red painted footsteps and the launch pad is getting closer. Now only a set of double doors, another right turn and the welcome signs to your choice of spacecraft, Varian or Electra? Continue on to Varian and check for delays on launch of both machines. Only 10 minutes for your carrier today but we know that could change. First put your ticket in the blue box so they know you're here and ready to go.

Bid the time of day to fellow travellers, some new, some veterans, some occupied reading books or magazines, others simply with their thoughts, and the more adventurous struggling with a jigsaw puzzle. Anything to keep their minds off the clock and the delay notices.

One hour to launch, start preparing for the journey. Follow the rules for flights; empty bowels and half an hour later take on board 600 ml of water. Hope that gas levels are within limits and wait for announcement to be called forward to the staging post.

Others get their calls forward; mine must be soon. Relief, I am summoned. Lift-off is imminent; nod to those still patiently waiting and proceed around the corner and remove my shoes. Keep calm, it is going to be okay, you've done this many times already, so no pressure. But there's always the possibility of a last-minute technical hitch. Think of NASA's Challenger fatal launch.

The radioactive warning has just turned from red to amber and launch staff enter the launch pad, and seconds later the previous astronaut walks out smiling. My name is called again, and I am accompanied in.

Remove trousers and lay on the launch bench, feet in foot slots, knees slightly raised. The technicians check my predetermined tattoo marks fit with the path of the rays. Cool hands move my hips in place while the launch pad is positioned for blast off. All is okay and technicians bid me safe journey and retire outside the danger zone.

I'm on my own now. The only sound is the whirring of the apparatus. This is it, there's no going back. Silence except for last minute positioning of my flight simulator, two clicks of the launch pad. Arms crossed with hands under armpits and I am away.

The huge arms start their orbit in a clockwise, slow yet smooth trajectory around me, stopping after one revolution with a small click. A short wait followed by another complete revolution. Each second my life's journey is flowing out of me. Old friends and acquaintances flash through my mind until the unit clicks back into its launch position.

The sound of the safety barrier opening and the welcome voice of the launch assistant. I am at my journey's end for today and they lower me down to table level and I am free to go. Another journey, another day. Out to the sunshine and view the hill to climb and return to this world - simple buses and cars. Gravity is a wonderful thing.

The schoolchildren in the bus shelter, glued to iPhones and pads, don't notice me as I pass by. I have just been to places beyond their imagination while they play with simple earthly creations made to fill their minds and gain the approval of others.

I have passed over the huge expanse of water in the Sea of Tranquillity; seen Jupiter's many moons – Europa, Ganymede and several others; marvelled at the icy rings on Saturn and the ancient rivers on Mars. I would love to visit Pluto, but it is not available on day trips.

The Christmas Tree

The doorbell rang just as Gordon was struggling with the long, recently delivered cardboard box to put it into the loft. Cursing to himself he shoved the box into the opening and followed it with the stepladder and shut the hatch.

'Can you get that Gordon?' June called from the lounge where she was putting the finishing touches to the tree decorations. It was quite remarkable how, after all these years, she managed to make an order sound like a request and worst still, ask him to do something that he was about to do of his own volition anyway.

Smoothing his hair as he went, he approached the front door and opened it with a smile that Richard Nixon would have been proud of.

Janet, his sister-in-law, and Freddie, her husband stood there, huge friendly grins creasing their faces as they both wished him 'Merry Christmas' but then stepped inside almost as if the door had opened automatically and Gordon wasn't there.

He closed the door and followed them into the lounge where June and Janet were hugging each other as though they had not seen one another for an eternity, when in fact it was less than a week ago that they went shopping together.

'That ain't a real tree,' spouted Freddie as though he had made some important discovery.

'I don't recall saying it was,' replied Gordon, more than a little indignant, as if he had been caught out in some form of cheating. 'The real ones are too messy, and we got fed up with all the needles they shed.' He offered in his defence.

'Why, have you taken over cleaning duties then Gord?'

He looked at Freddie, who had broken out into that ridiculous laugh that always set Gordon's teeth on edge, and the two ladies joined in the chorus of laughter. The trio had the look of the front row of a Michael McIntyre matinee.

'I'll go and make some tea,' Gordon said, retreating to the kitchen where, above the noise of the electric jug boiling, he could still hear their inane guffaws.

'What's that noise Gordon? Gordon, wake up.' June was feeling around the other side of the bed and panic set in when she found it was empty. She leapt out of bed, grabbing her dressing gown as she rushed into the lounge.

All the lights were on and Gordon was sitting amongst the artificial Christmas tree that lay in pieces all around him. Baubles and decorations were strewn around the floor as though a mad bear had broken in.

For a split second, June was speechless. She thought, no hoped, she was dreaming, for indeed it was a nightmare scene. Then she screamed 'What on earth have you done Gordon? That tree took me bloody hours to decorate.'

He just looked at her, tears streaming down his face. 'You and your bloody family have laughed at me for the last time you miserable bitch. You know it was all your idea to buy a bloody plastic tree. It was you who complained every minute of the day about the dropping needles, but you joined in and laughed at me with those stupid sods. Well, now you've really got something to clear up, haven't you?'

Playing on Grass

Monday morning, and slightly unwell from the previous night's encounter with her ex-boyfriend, Carole pulled up at the traffic lights and watched the windscreen wipers disperse the now steady rain.

Alerted by the car behind her that the lights had turned green she started move off very slowly in an attempt to teach the impatient prick a lesson. How dare they; and her a police officer. There's always one she thought, shaking her head in disapproval, hoping the driver could see her annoyance and notice the uniform.

As she pulled away, she noticed three figures in the small park by the intersection, fighting in the middle of the grass. She speeded up, took the next left turn, pulled up somewhat untidily and jumped out of the car.

As she ran across the road yelling for them to stop, she realised she should've asked for back-up being as her prey were three grown men. However, the two who were fighting stopped and looked in her direction.

'Just what d'you think you're doing fighting in this park?' she managed to blurt out after a sudden, unexpected run across the road. Reaching for her radio she realised it was back in the car. 'Well what is going on? Why are you fighting? She began to size them up, wondering if she hadn't bitten off more than she could chew: it wasn't the first time. They were all dressed in grey Pakistani shalwar kameezes. The two who had been fighting with one another were covered with wet patches, grass stains and mud.

The one who appeared to have been little more than a spectator was the first to speak, removing his brown cloth cap, the type favoured by people from Pakistan and Afghanistan.

'We sorry madam but we did not think we were making nuisance and are thinking this padang is open to anyone.'

'It is, but not for fighting at seven o'clock in the morning, for heaven's sake. What is wrong that you needed to fight with one another. What brought this on?'

'Please madam we were not fighting,' this from the tallest of the three and one of the wrestlers. 'Please, we are wrestling in friendly way. You can see that Ahmed here is not injured. We do this back home in the Punjab. It is sporting only madam.'

Carole was relieved that they seemed harmless but was still bemused about the timing of their 'wrestling'.

'Can I see your passports please – all of you.' She felt a need to take control of the situation although their innocent excuses made it seem that her intervention was probably unnecessary.

'We sorry but our passports are on our boat. Captain-Sahib is not letting us leave the boat with them. He is thinking we not returning.' He reached into his breast pocket and pulled out a somewhat dog-eared Seaman's Pass and offered it to her. The others followed suit.

Carole was now missing her radio even more, as she had no knowledge of procedures in such circumstances, having only been transferred to Southampton three months previously. She pondered going back with the permits and checking via radio if what they said rang true and decided against it. It was raining quite steadily now, and she wished she'd never started this investigation.

'So, you are all from a boat in the harbour?'

'Yes,' the spectator one implored, 'Please madam do not get us into trouble as maybe we lose our jobs. Captain-Sahib is very angry man if we cause any troubles. He always warning us before he let us ashore.'

She looked at each pass, trying to identify each of them in turn with the photos. But if she was brutally honest, she was unable to because they all looked remarkably similar, and the passes were in poor condition and the photos badly creased. Best to wrap this up, Carole was mulling over in her mind, not to mention getting out of this rain.

'Okay, but before I let you off, I want to know why the heck you choose to come here in the park at this time in the morning?'

This remark brought smiles to each of their faces, and they started to look relieved for the first time since she yelled at them.

'Please madam it was the rain and the chance to play our wrestling on this grass. We have been on the boat for long time and miss the feel of real grass under our feet for so long and no place for friendly wrestle on our boat. We very sorry if we did some crime.'

Carole handed the passes back to them. 'Alright but you had better find some grass more private than right here in the city centre. Understood?'

The trio beamed broad smiles again and nodded in unison. The two fighters put their sandals back on, each placing their hand over their heart and saying profuse 'thank yous' before turning away and walking towards the main road.

Carole, relieved in spite of being quite wet, turned back to her car shaking her head, and smiled for the first time during the encounter.

The Flying Bedstead

There is probably no darker place on earth than a jungle-fringed minor road on a moonless night in West Africa. The Land Rover's headlights created an orange tunnel for me to follow as I negotiated the twists and turns the road makers had created, following the path of least resistance through this tropical labyrinth.

I was on a short journey north from Ughelli to pick up Beth, the local Peace Corps schoolteacher. We had met a couple of weeks back at the market and our friendship had blossomed from there. I guess the similarity in our ages both in years and length of service in Nigeria was the main factor in us hitting it off so well. I had invited her to dinner at our base camp. After driving for fifteen minutes, I was startled by a loud bang, which I assumed signalled a puncture. A swift kick on each tyre showed no puncture, so thinking it must have been a rock thrown up underneath, I climbed back in and continued on.

Turning into Beth's compound the outside security lights illuminated the front of the truck and showed that the nearside windscreen was shattered. I pulled up and went round to inspect the damage. There was a dent in the top left-hand corner of the windscreen frame. Some bugger must have a thrown a rock at me.

By now Beth had joined me. 'Hi Gary, what are you looking at?'

'Oh, hi Beth, sorry. Some sod has thrown a rock at me and busted the windscreen, look at that – could have killed me if it had gone through the side window.'

'Wow – you were lucky. That is so unlike them, the local village people have been nothing but nice to me. Anyway, come on, let's get down to your place, I'm starving'.

'Gee it really is dark out here Gary.' She patted my knee consolingly and I was beginning to feel better when suddenly the headlights picked up a makeshift barrier across the road and a small crowd of people.

A man came running up to the side of the truck and shouted, 'You crazy driver you have killed one lady from our village.'

Several others joined in, yelling at the tops of their voices and waving machetes. I was very afraid as situations like this could easily end up with us being attacked.

Fortunately, they recognised Beth and she quickly calmed them down. 'Just a minute,' she implored. 'Where is the lady's body?'

'She be taken to the hospital in town.' The man who had taken the role of spokesman spat back at her.

'But I thought she was dead.' Beth reasoned calmly. I was just too scared trying to fathom out how I had hit someone without seeing them and all of seven feet off the ground.

I found my voice and suggested to him to get in, and we would take him and help the victim to the hospital. The barrier was removed, and we drove off back down the road. Moments later we came across the woman on a bicycle being wheeled along by two men.

She had a nasty jagged gash to the right side of her forehead that was bleeding profusely but otherwise she appeared in one piece. We helped her into the rear passenger seat along with one of her helpers and headed down to Ughelli.

The rest of the evening was something that only a person who has lived in Nigeria in the sixties would hope to understand. Being Saturday evening, the hospital was relatively quiet; the doctor was friendly, understanding and confident that the wound was superficial requiring a 'few' stitches and an overnight stay. It was explained I would be expected to pay her expenses.

Next, I was summoned to the police station, where it turned out the chief had gone home. I would be required to make a statement and then return at 8 o'clock the following morning.

I recited carefully what had happened to a sergeant who relayed it to a constable who was sat in front of an ancient typewriter. He typed in a manner that gave the impression he questioned the actual existence and location of each and every letter key.

At a quarter to midnight, we were free to resume our evening. The servants had saved us some cold food which we ate in the silence of the now empty dining room. The evening that I had looked forward to for days was ruined, and there was nothing other than to take Beth home.

Sunday morning, straight after breakfast, I had a driver take me to the police station. There I had the most distasteful three hours bartering for legal closure of the accident.

The police chief was fat and horrible; sitting behind this huge desk covered with a mixture of various paperwork, dirty cups and two telephones that rang incessantly but were never answered. Other matters could wait; the thought of a hard cash settlement hung in the air. He never spoke directly to me, choosing to utter short grunts in Yoruba to a sergeant who then translated these utterances into lengthy questions.

On the occasions that he looked directly at me it was the look of a spider enjoying the sight of a trapped fly – supper guaranteed. The buttons on his khaki shirt strained to contain his large belly and dark patches began to show at his armpits.

I felt helpless and very nervous, deeply afraid and defenceless; ashamed of both my alleged misdemeanour and yet at a loss to understand how it happened.

Eventually after two or three hours of this circus it transpired the chief had decreed that I was to pay a fine of fifty Nigerian pounds for reckless driving. Furthermore, I should settle the woman's hospital fees, provide transportation back to her village and buy her a new bed.

'A new bed?' I exclaimed, 'why on earth should I buy her a new bed?'

My driver, who had been present throughout the proceedings, whispered to me that the woman had been transporting a metal bed frame on her head last night. Hearing my approach, she must have stepped back off the road into the jungle leaving the bed frame protruding out into the road. It had been struck by my Land Rover with such force that it spun her out of sight into the bush injuring her head in the process.

In Africa everything eventually makes sense. Acquiring the patience required to reach the answer is the biggest hurdle for the newcomer.

He's My Brother

The sound of lightly breaking waves and the rustle of the early morning breeze brought scant comfort to Morag. The seawater snaking up to her outstretched legs caused her to retreat once more.

The memory of the church and those officers in uniforms with those ridiculous red trousers and spurs made her shiver with impotent rage. She had looked after her baby brother safely for eighteen years. They couldn't manage three. He returned home in an oak box draped with the union flag.

He promised he would be protected inside an armoured vehicle, when in fact only the rubber sole of a boot separated him from the enemy – an IED. She recalled the tears and arguments she had with him and their parents, begging him not to join the army. All in vain, and now he was gone. If only they had listened.

Cape Wrath: she drove here directly from her brother Ross's funeral, avoiding the wake. It had been his favourite place name from the shipping forecast. A game they played as children; her choice was Fastnet. She had searched her mind for any scrap that she could remember about him, his likes and dislikes. For now, the rugged beauty and isolation provided the calm she craved. Next, she would travel south to Glasgow to the next Celtic match, and imagine Ross was beside her, yelling for the green stripes to win. Just to shout would allow her to expel some of that anger mixed with regret that fermented inside her.

She stood up, brushing the sand from her bottom, and walked slowly back to the hotel. In the dining room she was the first guest in for breakfast. She avoided what she took as the silent flirtation from the hazel eyes of the young waiter. There was no room in her life for a man this close to her loss.

The Masta Mak

Reading Joseph Conrad's novel Heart of Darkness, the description of Marlow's progress into the interior of the African jungle reminded me of the year I spent as a Masta Mak or land surveyor, in the then Australian Trust Territory of Papua, New Guinea.

My arrival at Port Moresby airport in January 1969 is still fresh in my mind. The airport was little more than a huge open tin shed, alive with the traffic of expatriate Australians hoping to make their fortune in this neighbouring country north of their homeland across the Coral Sea.

It was like being in a fishing pond sprinkled with floats; a mixture of Akubra and Stetson hats intermingled with an array of floppy versions and the occasional seeding dandelion-heads of black globes of fuzzy hair reminiscent of actors from the stage show Hair. The blight of the baseball cap had not yet penetrated the eastern hemisphere, so Oz rules reigned supreme in headgear.

The year turned out to be fascinating and physically challenging. Though my stay represented only a thread in the tapestry of my life, 52 years later it still looms large in my mind. I have no notes or personal diaries and only a few black and white photos to draw upon. The rest is from memory.

This was the year that Neil Armstrong became the first man to walk on the moon, yet in some New Guinea villages I visited, often probably one of the few white men to do so, conditions did not seem to me far removed from the Stone Age.

In late November of that year, this project was to be my last assignment. Travelling around that remarkable country - a wild, rough, yet wonderful place with a long history of tribal in-fighting, cannibalism, exotic birds of paradise and a breath-taking string of islands and volcanoes. During the year the projects had been many and varied, from the coastal forests of eastern Papua, the Southern

Highlands around Lake Kutubu, the wildness of the island of Bougainville and now here in New Britain. Later I was to sail around the Trobriand Islands with their pretty girls and grass skirts, a truly South Pacific scene.

I was accommodated in a variety of places; villages, plantations, missions and forestry camps to name but a few. From time to time and by contrast, nights isolated under a simple shelter, a tarpaulin slung over a freshly cut wood frame and a canvas stretcher bed between me and the forest floor. I staggered up forested hills and mountains, hacking my way through untamed jungle. Many times a day I waded across streams and rivers, sometimes having to dive in from the back of a speedboat and swim ashore.

At this latitude the sun disappears in the early evening, so bedtime came early and most evenings were spent lying underneath a mosquito net reading by the beam of a flashlight. As the sun went down, the insects began their evening chorus to sing me to sleep. Working in isolation and existing with no means of communication meant there was no lifeline. Often it was a question of literally thinking on one's feet in addition to accepting local advice and weighing up the wisdom thereafter.

Orders, requests and directions were a struggle, conversations a mixture of simple English and the lingua franca of New Guinea, Tok Pisin, a wonderful conglomeration of mutilated English with sprinklings of German and Malay. In Papua the language was Police Motu and throughout the country over 850 local dialects that isolated the foreign traveller even further. Not being that proficient in the language often caused much pain and exasperation especially searching for nouns and nomenclature. As a land surveyor I was simply known as Masta Mak – a white man who makes marks. Given names were of little consequence; occupational definition was all that was needed when you are the only outsider.

I met an extraordinary diversity of people, from the primitive villager eking out an existence in horrifying levels of poverty and hardship to dedicated missionaries and teachers offering help and assistance. Then there were expatriate entrepreneurs, often no more than bandits who took from everyone. But wherever my journeys took me, like so many visitors to this unusual and remote country I experienced the kindness of strangers; here was the divergence from Conrad's writing.

The bubble-like chopper took off from the Australian agricultural project in a settlement called Keravat, less than an hour by a dirt road from the New Britain capital, Rabaul, and flew to a remote village in a region known as the Bainings in the Gazelle Peninsula. The Bainings are a challenging, rugged area of mountainous tropical forest in the east of the island. There was only the carrying capacity for a pilot and two passengers and very little else, especially flying in a region where weather conditions and topography are so changeable and challenging.

Due to the lateness of the day and the need for the helicopter to return to its base in Rabaul before nightfall, we hastily landed on the edge of the village. My patrol box was unceremoniously unloaded; my boss simply shook my hand and wished me good luck before the pilot whisked him away. Now it was me and my tin box. Facing me was a group of villagers, a mixture of ages and sexes, staring at me rather like a herd of wildebeest would regard a water source wondering if it contained a crocodile. After the excitement of the helicopter, I think I was a bit of a let-down.

Once the noise and backdraft of the departing aircraft ceased, one of those awkward silences ensued until the village headman stepped forward and offered to shake my hand. Moments like these came flooding back to my memory as I progressed through the chapters of Heart of Darkness. After a brief introduction I asked if they had a Haus Kiap - a hut that is kept empty in most villages to accommodate visiting administration Patrol Officers or Kiaps as they were known in Tok Pisin. They did. Having explained my business was that of a Masta Mak, would he get 20 men ready to work with me the next day? Again, the reply was positive, and he looked both stern and pleased.

Having smiled at everyone and putting on an air of self-assurance I certainly didn't feel, I ordered two boys to pick up my patrol box and show me to my hut. The magic patrol box was a substantial oblong tin box complete with a lock-hasp and two loop handles either end sufficient for a pole to be inserted along the length of the box so that it could be transported shoulder high by two bearers. It contained my clothes, blanket, mosquito-net, tinned food, books and various papers.

The village was situated on a cleared ridge top and housed a hundred or so people. Families lived in round huts made from basic timber felled by axe, cleaned by machete and covered with leaf and reed-matting; they didn't have any windows and just a partially concealed open doorway. The floors were bare earth and in the centre was an open fire from which the smoke simply permeated through the roof. From the outside the village looked like a series of eerie, large smoking mushrooms. Each hut measured about six metres in diameter and three metres high in the centre. The occupants slept on rush mats on the ground around an open fire which accounted for the occasional badly disfigured person – the result of accidentally rolling into the fire while sleeping in childhood.

The Haus Kiap was quite different; rectangular and built on stilts about fifty centimetres off the ground. It measured about five by three metres and less than two metres high at the central ridge. The door was secured by a cheap little padlock that was quickly unlocked by a young boy, and my box was placed inside the bare hut.

The main difference, besides the shape and raised floor, was the fact that it had a small, barred window on each wall. Once I entered, every window and the doorway were jam-packed with shiny black faces eagerly watching every move I made. The opening of my patrol box created little gasps of delight and I could feel the energy being expended by my audience vying for the best view of its contents. I set about making my bed for the night and preparing a meal; each movement gave cause for giggles and muted comments from my audience. Thankfully daylight was fading and gradually my audience drifted away to their own huts and only one boy remained to act as my personal assistant. Though tired from the journey, sleep did not come to me easily that night.

The next day I awoke immediately on sunrise; having no means of closing the windows, sunlight shone straight into the hut. Shortly afterwards the lad acting as my houseboy came in with a welcome mug of hot water that tasted of smoke. I used it to make a cup of instant coffee. Ablutions would have to wait until I could deduce how to handle my celebrity status; always an awkward situation when your every move is monitored in daylight by the entire village, particularly by the youngsters.

One of the main problems of living in a village built on a ridge top is the total lack of any running water. It all had to be hauled by the women, young and old, from the river at the bottom of the hill. There was a certain amount stored in earthenware pots around the outside of the huts which would catch the run-off from the roofs when it rained. These were also topped up with hand-carried amounts from the river below.

Suffice it to say that with life in remote parts on foot-patrols, personal hygiene was minimal in both content and priority. Very often it didn't stretch much beyond teeth-cleaning, another custom that was found fascinating by my hosts. However, the occasional monsoonal downpours were a welcome relief when they occurred, especially at the end of the day, and I would strip to my underpants and luxuriate in God's shower – this was also regarded as yet another odd practice and a popular must-see for everyone. For them, getting drenched was the result of rain, but to purposely stand in it seemed very odd indeed.

Once I showed signs that I was ready for my intended project, the headman came to me and told me that he had organised the 20 men I required. It had been necessary to go to the next village to make up the number as there was an insufficient amount of men in this village. He also explained to me that it was necessary to leave some of their own men behind during our work outside the village as protection for the women and children.

The group was assembled and stood expectantly awaiting to be told what was required of them. These instructions had to be painstakingly translated from me, whose language skills in Tok Pisin were matched only by my patience, then by the headman into the village dialect. I explained that our task was to locate six or so suitable locations around the region, clear the site of immediate trees and vegetation and construct helicopter landing pads using the wood that had been cleared in the process. These points would be chosen to locate survey stations for aerial mapping purposes which could be later occupied quickly and efficiently by helicopter transportation.

Each point would be on an elevated position capable of both observing and being visible in certain directions in order for the survey to run. After a brief headcount and check that each man was suitably equipped with all four limbs plus an axe and a machete, an attempt was then made to demonstrate how to construct a landing pad using a scale model, painstakingly constructed from small twigs. It didn't take long for me to realise that the only persons to benefit from this were me and the boy helping me to collect suitable twigs and fashion them.

The rest of the day was spent in planning my proposed positions and generally trying my best to interpret the aerial photos. The biggest headache was to decide on the most economical route and getting some ideas from my newly acquired workers proved difficult. They did their best to help, eager to start on this, their first ever paid occupation, at the going rate of one Australian dollar per man per day!

After two weeks or so we managed with great difficulty, descending and climbing hills, often in torrential rain, stumbling through streams and the occasional river, to position four sites complete with helipads. The one saving grace in this process was that the forest was not unduly thick and virtually all the trees were softwoods, many of which looked more like suspended space-rockets held in place by their roots that sprout about a metre off the ground, which made felling an easy task.

However, the project had fallen behind in time, and due to a shortage of supplies it would be necessary to leave at the completion of the fourth site. The decision was met with considerable dismay by the men at the thought of losing their recently acquired celebrity, and of course a dollar a day. The last afternoon was spent paying each man his hard-earned wages. With heavy heart, the following morning I set off with two fit young men to carry my patrol box on yet another trek, which I was assured could be achieved in one day following a well-used walking track.

The going was slow and taxing, not least because I had developed a really bad cold and I can honestly say it was the thought of a return to relative civilisation at my immediate destination, a Catholic mission on the coast, that kept me going that day, literally one foot after the other. Late afternoon the small footpath we were following ran into a volcanic-cinder road cleared for hauling the timber to the Mission, a major sawmill as I was to learn. Two agonising hours later, no longer afforded the shelter of the tree cover from the burning sun, my destination finally came into view.

Staggering into the Mission itself I must have looked a rather forlorn sight. All I can recall after a brief introduction was being given a towel, shown a bathroom and bedroom, and after a quick shower falling into a death-like sleep until the following morning. A real bed – nothing could have been appreciated more. The sleep made me feel like a new man; it is quite amazing how one night's proper rest in a comfortable bed can have such rehabilitating effects. I got up, dressed and went to meet my new hosts who had simply accepted me without any question the previous day. This was not my first experience of the hospitality of the Roman Catholic Church. This particular one was staffed by German nationals comprising of a Father, two Brothers and several Sisters.

Breakfast was at a real table with chairs and talking in plain English was a welcome change. My hosts were gracious and appeared to be interested in listening to the purpose of my project and my experiences. Outside, the whole setting was as tranquil as it was exotic, with the Mission comprising of several single storey buildings in unfussy well-maintained gardens and neatly cut grass lawns leading down to the water's edge. Further to the south-east sat Mount Ulawan, an active huge volcano majestically looking down on us – it had been given, as with all the volcanoes in the territory, a family name. Ulawan had been christened 'The Father' and was thankfully asleep.

All that remained now was to get myself back to Rabaul once passage on a passing trading boat could be arranged. My luck was in, since a suitable vessel was scheduled in two days' time as a delivery of goods and foodstuffs was expected, and the Sister-Doctor who wanted to go to Rabaul for some Christmas shopping had already booked a passage. It was agreed that I would accompany her.

Three days later the boat duly arrived and unloaded the cargo of supplies. I bade farewell to all the staff that morning, thanked them profusely for their kind hospitality and I boarded the boat along with my fellow passenger, the Sister-Doctor.

The Captain and the First Mate were both mixed-race men from Rabaul, and the Sister was well acquainted with both of them. Apart from their frequent trips to the Mission, she knew them and many of their peers through the fact that the Catholic Church in New Britain looked after, and in many cases educated, the vast majority of mixed-race children.

It was yet another of the conundrums of prejudice that was ingrained in a region whose everyday life was heavily influenced by tribal instincts; where people who lived but walking distance away could be, and often were, regarded as the enemy. So a person who could be easily identified as not belonging to any individual tribe had problems beyond mere dialect. Unfortunately, this meant that the offspring of mixed relationships faced difficulties of not really belonging to either race and it was here the missionaries stepped in and bridged that gap.

The Captain made us very comfortable, well at least as best as he could in the rather confined, small bridge area – the boat was probably no more than thirty metres long. But they managed to serve us some basic food, washed down with a bottle or two of South Pacific Lager, the Territory's local and much quaffed popular beer. The voyage again created similarities with Conrad's novel. A diverse group on board a small boat, albeit at sea rather than on a river, but the feeling was there.

It was certainly a strange situation for me to be sitting on the deck of a small trading ship and sharing a bottle of beer with a Catholic nun, chatting about life and things in general as though we were old friends. It was a very interesting insight into the life and

126

thoughts of a woman who had dedicated her life to the people of a totally alien culture. Most interesting was her honest appraisal of the relationship of the missionaries with their parishioners. One thing she was brutally frank about was that, living in a part of the world where the practice of pay-back killings was an everyday fact of life, she felt that if insurrection ever took hold of the local tribes, the missionaries would probably be in the front line of casualties. The work and sacrifice they had made and the Christian message they had preached would not save them.

As darkness approached, the captain came out and said that as there was no passenger accommodation, the Sister-Doctor could have his bunk. She thanked him for this and a little later when he was out of earshot, quietly asked me to sleep immediately outside of his cabin door. She explained that though she knew both men well, as they had been drinking beer, she did not trust them. Naturally I was quite happy to do so and bunked down on the deck with my head against the cabin door.

We docked in Rabaul harbour the following morning and the Sister-Doctor and I disembarked. It didn't look or feel like we were approaching Christmas but nonetheless we both wished each other the season's greetings and went our separate ways. I found a phone and called my colleagues who were based an hour or so away in Kerevat and asked them to come and pick me up.

In the meantime, I headed for a barbers' shop. It was quite early in the morning and I must have been his first customer of the day. The Australian proprietor looked pleasantly surprised when I asked him to shave off my beard completely and cut my rather long hair right down to a 'college-boy' style. Both the shave and the haircut were like a tonic after a year of not being at all concerned with my appearance. My colleagues were impressed with my new clean-cut look when they arrived.

The only person who was not so delighted with my return from the wilds was my boss, who was underwhelmed by the fact that the exercise only achieved four out of the six intended sites. He and I never ever hit it off over the entire year, ever since I got lost on my first night out in Moresby. I had been forced to ring him to get some directions home late in the night.

The decision was made to return to the Bainings to continue the survey and find a way of combining my (inadequate) four pads with a site in another large village that I thought I was able to see from one of my new sites. We flew directly to this position which was easy to find because of its size – it was a big village that I imagine had grown as a result of having a resident missionary.

Landing was easy because there was a football pitch in the centre of the village on which to land. As usual the whole village turned out to see us and we were celebrities once again. What was most surprising was the fact there was no sign of the missionary, so I enquired if he was indeed still here. The children all nodded in the affirmative and pointed to a wooden house built on stilts behind the end goalposts. They then followed me excitedly pointing out the hut lest I should lose my way.

It seemed rather odd having landed within 200 metres of this house, with all the noise and dust that a helicopter makes, that the occupant did not come out to greet me, but he didn't. So I walked over, climbed the steps up to the front door and knocked. Moments later the door opened and a priest politely invited me in. I explained the purpose of our visit and asked would he mind if we used the football pitch as a survey position, to which he replied, 'by all means' and that was the extent of our meeting. I was dying to ask why he showed little interest in our landing, but it seemed inappropriate.

Next, we flew back to the village where I had stayed before, and our arrival caused just as much excitement as the previous time. Once the rotor blades of the helicopter came to a stop I walked over and called to the village headman to come forward. A hush rippled through the villagers and they started to back away from me, so I called one or two by name. Hearing my voice and me knowing their names caused them to recoil from me. They were spooked and one or two turned and literally fled as if in fear of their lives.

It took several moments before the realisation dawned on me – they didn't recognise me without a beard and long hair. It was only after several assurances that they started to laugh and joke. They were totally amazed and kept asking how I could leave them as an old man and return a week later as a boy. It was too much to take in. It was a fitting end to a year of living and working in this, one of the world's last frontiers.

Dawn at Wadi Affez

'Tomorrow, Inshallah, you will die Ingleezi.' The tall one of my captors who I call Lurch grinned, showing tobacco-stained, misshapen teeth. Staring passively at this prick who insisted on calling me 'Ingleezi', when a voice in my head screamed 'knock his ugly face in,' was the ultimate state of wretchedness.

He closed the ill-fitting door to a scraping judder of uneven wooden slats grating the sand on the concrete base. He had left various taunts hanging in the air every evening over the past six months. It was his macabre way of leaving me disorientated in that confined, solitary existence where the crossover from day to night was imperceptible.

'So, young Boyer what do you intend to do with your life when you leave school next year?'
It was just like old Satchmo Snelzic to start asking questions like this when my only thought was to get away for my first date with Trish Andrews.
'Not really given it much thought.' As nothing worth remembering had happened in Bendigo since the Gold Rush two hundred bloody years ago, getting out of that dead hole was my main thought. 'I think I'd like to be a reporter' was all I could offer.

London 2015
It all started in a pub with one of those stupid discussions that turn into arguments, this time with my wife Trish and some of her schoolteacher mates.

Much as I tried to keep my temper during these friendly chats, what with this lot being so left-wing, I never succeeded. The worst was Kamal, a refugee from Iran, a physical education teacher who was sweet on Trish. The subject was Syria and how the West was not doing enough to rid the country of Assad, and why the UK didn't take in more refugees.

Knowing I didn't share the group's opinions, Trish ended up going to their gatherings without me. But late in the summer we were invited to a barbeque. It went well for a while until Kamal just started winding me up.

'So you're a journalist, Tom?'

'Correction. Lecturer in journalism.'

'You've never actually been to report on these wars that you seem to know all about?'

'That's right – I am not a war correspondent. But I'm considering resigning my job and heading to Syria as a freelance. Happy now?' There it was, out loud – for all to hear.

Survival guide for journalists
Part 1. *Be prepared*

The frightening sound of nearby small arms fire woke me with a start. My captor Lurch's last words had made sleep difficult. When my eyes closed all I could picture was his crooked teeth and the evil, mocking glint in his eyes. Now the bastards were firing their bloody guns just when I managed to fall asleep.

The stupid, misguided sods spent most of their time firing at sweet nothing, except when the cruel bastards felt the need to execute some poor bugger they had captured. Watching through a gap in the wall, I saw their enemies were mere kids in uniform. Their mothers would never know what had happened to them.

Oh Jesus, how I longed for a change of clothes, toothpaste, food without cinnamon or a night's sleep without these bloody shackles; to wake to the sound of galahs raiding dad's fruit trees; the smell of Trish's hair; to go bloody home.

Part 2. *Danger Zone*

Wide awake again, repeat the daily task of recalling my journey here; picking up details to use in an escape the first time the opportunity presents itself. It keeps me sane – almost.

'Do you, Thomas Edward, take Patricia Elizabeth to be your lawful wedded wife?' It was enough to make a man cry the way Trish looked that

day. Then only a short three years and a bit later she appeared to find the company of her colleagues, especially the Iranian PE teacher, preferable to mine.

Part 3. *War zones & conflict areas*

Keep it simple. Book a week's package holiday on the coast in Anatolia. The Turks in the bars were friendly and it was a heaven-sent opportunity to pick up a smattering of culture and lingo. Funny how politics was similar to the feeling in the UK, where they yearn for a Churchill-like saviour to rescue them from the European Union. This lot was dreaming of an Ataturk to gain them entry.

At the end of the week, first a bus to Ankara and then onto Diyarbakir. Travelling by bus was good preparation for what happened next, sort of artillery at dawn, as grandad recalled about Gallipoli.

A melting pot of cultures and suspicion. The effect of fanatical religion where a follower is either spying on a fellow believer or looking over his shoulder to see who might be questioning his level of reverence. The only thing everyone agreed on is their dislike of the Kurds.

Not being able to face another bus journey I joined a pick-up taxi. A big mistake. I'm not sure which was worse, the terrifying driving or the smells of my fellow passengers and their wares, some of it live, festooned around the roof and under our feet.

At a roundabout on the outskirts of Urfa I signalled the driver to stop outside a small hotel bearing a sign Touristic Hotel. After I'd checked in I discovered it was no more than a brothel, but a bed is a bed and I needed sleep, even though there were no sheets.

'Look Tom there is no way our marriage can survive if you go off to bloody Syria. It's bad enough living here in the UK where the kids are even worse than back home, the traffic drives me mad and every time I look out of the window it's pissing with rain.'

Plans & travelling alone

Two useful pieces of advice picked up in Diyarbakir from a French correspondent with Reuters: 'Never take the first offer of help and avoid locals who speak good English.'

No food was on offer at the hotel the next morning, so I checked out, walked into town and found a café where I had tea and pastries for my breakfast. The feeling of standing out like a sore thumb made me realise it wasn't wise to hang around. A few blocks away, in a small side street I came across a wizened bloke in a dirty flat cap leaning against a battered Nissan. After a conversation of mainly gesticulations, and sealed with a modest advance, he agreed to take me over the border that night. We would meet in the same street at sundown. The timing was perfect since the streets should be empty as the population would be indoors feeding.

The border

He was as good as his word, though the car was like riding a skateboard on the dirt road. He had obviously done the journey many times and was known by the guards on both sides of the border. The lack of formality was mind-boggling. There is tougher security at a Melbourne minor league footy game. The only requirement was to cross grubby palms with green. These guys didn't want written proof that anyone had passed through when they were on duty. The written word was as abhorrent to them as pig-meat, while the beauty of speech is its ability to dissipate like steam from a shisha pipe. The majority of the people passing through would disappear anyway, and ghost business suited their pocket perfectly.

The journey took forever, mainly because the road was so poor. The car had no functioning shock-absorbers and the old man drove on sidelights. I'm not sure if this was because of security, they didn't work, or he felt that it was preserving his battery. A little after ten, we entered a small Syrian town, deathly quiet at this hour.

The old guy dropped me outside a small hotel and drove away, silent with not so much as a wave or nod. I felt very alone and to be honest, shit-scared. It was necessary to think rationally, easier said than done walking along a darkened, unfamiliar street; but it was essential to take stock of my surroundings before bedding down

My mind started to play tricks. I imagined I was on the crosshairs of some hidden sniper's sights. Passing a couple of doors leaking cracks of light and catching my coat, it was easy to imagine the shards as marks of a laser sight. That, and the night chill made me shiver.

'Look Trish, this is something I've got to do. It won't be for ever and if it works I will have made a name for myself reporting something useful instead of the mundane crap that has been life to date. Also it will give you a chance to see what and more importantly who you want to be tied to, because right now it isn't clear.'

Hostage taking

The room in the 'hotel' was basic, but cleaner than the brothel in Urfa and quieter, without the continuous door slamming that changing bedfellows had caused back there. Remarkably, as a result sleep came quickly.

The next morning a knocking on my door and a croaking cry of 'Mista, Mista,' woke me.

For several seconds I couldn't recognise my surroundings, then I was able to manage an irritable 'Okay, I'm up – keep your shirt on.'

I slept fully clothed, being prepared to leg it, though I'd taken off my boots, so getting ready was quick. Donning my parka and grabbing my rucksack, I was out of the room in no time.

The morning desire to empty my bladder increased almost to the point of my pissing my pants, and it took considerable effort not to do so. It is difficult to know whether it was pride, or my guts turning to ice that kept my trousers dry. Standing there between me and the main door were three characters in military camouflage, their faces obscured by black balaclavas. Two of them were pointing AK47s directly at me. The hotel proprietor looked away; a fresh ragged cut on his face suggested why.

'Tom, I know things have been difficult but please come home. Where are you?' The line was crackly and made Trish's voice sound as though she was speaking from the bottom of a well.
'Don't worry, Trish. I'm still in Turkey and I'm okay. I'll be gone for a few more weeks and then I'll be home. I love you, take care.' I switched off the phone. It was the last time we spoke.

Part 4. *Recovery zone*

I woke again surprised by the absence of shackles scratching my dirty arms, still lying in my hut. They must have taken them off while I was sleeping. Someone in the group must want me to escape – they knew my family couldn't or wouldn't pay the ransom for my release and had decided to let me go. Or was it just to give them an excuse to shoot me?

But it was time to put my escape plan into action. Every time they had taken me outside I had noted the position of each bush, tent and building. The door was easy to prise open by slipping my fingers through the ill-fitting door frame. It was just possible to lift the latch up on the outside. It felt good to be able to move without the restriction of the shackles. I almost cried out 'Thank you'.

Dawn Breaks

Outside it was just beginning to get light. Always a good time, as my captors would be fast asleep having stayed up half the night. Now my boots. Never mind socks, speed is what matters. Slip the rucksack over my shoulder. Last look around and bring into focus in the half-light the camp layout: two shepherds' huts, three camouflaged tents and a few large bushes growing in the winter catchment area of the wadi.

Keep to the path leading along the well-trodden part of the wadi. There was a familiar feeling about the place, as though I had walked this route a hundred times before.

Isn't it strange how everything relates to childhood and the beauty of freedom? Back-packing at Falls Creek with dad. No stress, no responsibilities, just breathing the clean, fresh air.

End Game

'Wake up, Ingleezi, your time has come.' Lurch was standing over me; I could smell his fetid tobacco breath before my eyes opened. Now I almost retched as he lent closer and started to remove both sets of my shackles.

When he'd finished, he thrust a crumpled orange bundle at me and said, 'Put these on, Ingleezi. You need to look good in the video.'

Is this really the end? After rubbing my wrists to ease the burn of the shackles, with trembling hands I unwrapped the orange overalls. A shaft of dawn sunlight through the open door highlighted the colour. How strange, it was Trish's favourite colour – orange; the colour she'd chosen for our bridesmaids' dresses.

Ironic how I had longed for clean clothes. The lack of hygiene had been the hardest part to take. But my reprieve from dirt was going to be so short and not at all sweet. The overalls had been washed recently – they smelt of carbolic soap. Undoing the top button, I saw a large crimson stain inside the collar that had resisted the soap.

Looking for the Colonel

Stopping to unlatch my garden gate I was momentarily relieved to rest one of my shopping bags. As I pushed the gate open I dropped the bag, this time in shock because my front door was wide open and I could make out the shape of a person standing in the hallway.

It was the hat that caught my attention as I drew closer, and I realised I had seen it before, at the market on Tuesday. It was black, had seen better days and of the type I had seen Colonel Gaddafi wearing on the news. This wearer was a young Arab man with a pale face, dressed predictably in rather grubby white clothing.

As I approached the doorway I noticed he had a half empty bottle of milk in his hand and traces of milk on his upper lip. My mind was competing with anger, shock, fear and confusion as to what to do in this extraordinary situation.

'Excuse me young man, what on earth do you think you are doing in my house?'

'I didn't break your door, it was open missus,' he replied putting his left hand over his heart as a sign of apology, I presumed.

'You mean it was unlocked? I'm quite sure it was not open. I leave it unlocked for my son who will be here in a moment,' I lied. That must be the second time recently that I walked off to the shops leaving the house unlocked.

'Is that my bottle of milk you are drinking?'

'I didn't know it was yours, it was standing on the path outside the door. I'm sorry if you think I am bad man, but I was told at school that the Colonel said that when we came in from the oasis we could live in any house if the door was open.'

I didn't know whether to laugh or cry. Who on earth ever heard of such an excuse or explanation?

That was three months ago, and I'm still as undecided about the long-term answer to the conundrum created by this young Libyan called Omar Abdul Hamid walking into my house and now my life.

It transpired he was the son of a minor diplomat in the original Libyan embassy whose father mysteriously disappeared one day and left him effectively an orphan at the age of seventeen. It was at the time that Libya was in the throes of a devastating civil war and rumours were rife about the fate of all the members of the Libyan government and its followers, so Omar decided to make himself scarce.

His main excuse he offered me that day I found him in my front hallway was that he was looking for the Colonel. Gaddafi that is. What could I say in reply to that, I ask you? Apparently when his father was first called from his hometown of Sabha for service in Tripoli, he and others like him were told by the Colonel they could live anywhere they liked if the door of the house was open. It seemed my house fitted the bill for young Omar.

I hadn't the heart to tell him that Gaddafi's government had fallen and that the whereabouts of his dear Colonel was unknown. So then I faced a choice of throwing him out or offering him a place to stay. Looking at his forlorn face I chose the latter.

I covered the situation by telling everyone who noticed his presence that I had taken a lodger. It was all very simple. In the meantime, I scoured the internet for useful information that invariably offered me no help unless I contacted the authorities and made his presence known. Charities were also no help other than being a source of cheap clothing to put him in, which was essential if he was to avoid any awkward questions when outside the house.

It was at this point, having exhausted all the legal ways I could help this lad whom I had become attached to, that I hatched a plan. You see I lost both my husband Henry and 12-year-old son David nearly five years ago almost to the day that Omar came into my life. It was a sign that God had given me a new, replacement son.

My plan was very complicated in many ways, but the boys' similarity in ages made it simple in others. The fact that my late husband and I were both only children with no close relatives also helped.

First thing was to put the house on the market and start looking for a new home in Cornwall. Money was no object as the insurance money from Henry and David's accident was sitting in the bank, plus London property prices would go a long way in Cornwall.

Omar had everything he needed; a loving parent, a birth certificate and a National Insurance number; all he needed now was to remember that his name was David and his father's name was Henry.

Day Hawk

In the garden,
perfumes and colours abound.
By contrast,
a mullah's drab black on grey.
A crow has entered a paradise.
head bent forward,
deep in thought.

A mother nearby,
a breath of normality,
also in black.
She has no choice,
chides her gaggle of children,
for fear of offence.

What is he thinking?
Should *they* be here?
A new law perhaps,
yes, that's the answer.
How to word it?
To return solace,
in the garden.

*Note: Written from memories of seeing an Iranian cleric in a poet's garden
in Shiraz, Iran, circa 2000.*

No Direction Home

In the bottom drawer of my desk are ten passports, nine dead and one still alive and little used. A variety of issuing offices – starting in London, two in Cairo, then Singapore, Jakarta, Houston, Bangkok, Tripoli. Smudged ink stamps, illegible scribblings, sometimes in vivid green – a favourite in some Islamic states.

Memories come flooding back of time spent in immigration queues in the latest host country. A nervous look at the state of the airport, the immigration officer, other passengers.

Answering the ritual of questions; the luggage search, the removal of a magazine or simply a page ripped out because of an unsuitable article, picture or advertisement.

The last hurdle – released into the arrival hall. The scan for a friendly face. Is your name on a board or a scrap of cardboard being proffered? Offers for porters, taxis, hotels or moneychangers. Now no-one, you are alone. A stranger.

Try your best to look confident, even though the poster on the wall showing Colonel Gaddafi's attempt at a Churchillian V for victory has his hand round the wrong way.

The majority of pleasing memories are the simple ones. The kindness of strangers, to coin a phrase. The generosities of those who have little yet show their willingness to share. Their curiosity about how you do the simplest of things, eating, writing in a notebook, smoking a cigarette. Admiring your boots. Scrounging a pen or pencil.

Sometimes your celebrity status becomes tiresome. You just want to be left alone or ignored. Children are the worst, often with good reason for they have little to play with or occupy their growing minds. They have the tenacity of a sticky fly, and any attempt to shoo them away has the opposite effect and a game has been unintentionally started.

To be discovered in a small restaurant in a rural Thai village by an entire school of children as they finish their school day. If only you possessed the Nirvana of a mystic scholar. Look at your plate, don't return a stare even though the little boy or girl is willing you to look back at them.

The delicate young Thai waitress comes to your rescue from the goose that has started to attack. She grabs it by the neck and kicks it with bare feet.

Watching the fisherman balance on his small dugout canoe and cast his net out into River Niger while his young son keeps the craft calmly abreast of the current. The absolute silence and the pleasure of eating a slice of sweet papaya even though the cook has cut it with the same knife as he used on the onions he was preparing for dinner.

You have robbers in England? They get nearly 3 million pounds from a train? Wonderful sir – too much.

Entering a clearing on a vast Queensland farm at the end of a hot, tiring workday and spotting the aerobatic display of a male brolga attempting to woo a hen. Frustrating that your local helper, who has seen it all before, is not interested and longing for a cold beer before dinner.

Hey Pete this guy's a Pom. I know he's a good guy. Well best shoot him before he goes bad like the rest!

The companionship of a group of Punjabi workers sitting down and sharing a fiery potato and spinach dish straight from the tiffin carrier and spooned with torn pieces of rough chapatti warmed on an open fire. Afterwards a small snooze, cut short by someone yelling that they've spotted the presence of a snake.

What are those conical heaps by the houses Malik? That's bullshit sir.

Finding your battery is dead after bathing at a beach on the Gulf of Suez on a Friday afternoon. A kind Egyptian gentleman in a new BMW is happy to come to the rescue with a jump cable.

Is this place safe? A gunman killed 5 and injured 1 in this very hotel last week! What are we doing here? It's safe now.

Reporting to a rather simple Libyan policeman in an oasis in the Great Sand Sea of Calanscio; he comes bounding down the steps of his police station with such gusto he loses his step and tumbles. His hat disappears under my pickup and when I retrieve it for him, he is so grateful he forgets what he asked me to report for. We shake hands and I leave before he remembers.

Why do you only have one Libyan on your crew? I'm not sure – I guess the desert is not that attractive to graduates.

Sitting after lunch in the company's Jakarta office we are alerted by a mayday call from the radio. An American sailor is trying to spell out the name of his hijacked vessel, the MV Mayaguez, to the maritime radio operator in Manila. To help the situation we speak to the distraught sailor and alert the American embassy. In coming days, it becomes the last action of the Vietnam War when President Ford sends in troops to secure the release of the Mayaguez.

What do you think your government will do? If I had my way we'd blast them out of the water. In reality? Probably nothing.

Quietly working along a survey traverse in the Sinai Desert my heart almost stops when a huge Israeli transport plane flies just a few hundred feet over our heads. The backdraft all but knocks me over. Seemingly they were practising low level flying in preparation for the rescue mission of the hostages in Entebbe.

God gives nuts to monkeys with no teeth.

Landing in error by helicopter on the Somali side of the border in the Ogaden region of Ethiopia, we are promptly arrested and later handed over to the Somali military. Flown to Mogadishu and incarcerated in a large 'safe house' in the residential part of the city. We receive regular visits from the American, British and Ethiopian Vice-Consuls. A Somali brigadier, Kenneth Kaunda's doppelganger, gives us daily assurances. Nobody knows what to do with us. After two weeks they take us to the airport having booked us on a flight to Nairobi.

What's up; don't you guys like kidneys? They have given us their best for breakfast.

A rather sombre moment, one night fast asleep in my bed in the town of Sfax in Tunisia my phone rings and a voice says, 'You are American. You are not a friend of the Arab people and we will kill you.' Startled, I protested that I was neither of these two accusations. It did not make for a very comfortable night's sleep that night and for many after.

My collie-cross Brandy is happy – he is now allowed to sleep upstairs.

Taking a flight on an Air Niugini Skyvan from a remote airstrip I was taken aback that a large cassowary is trussed up in the rear seat wearing army boots. The pilot explained its owner had paid full fare for the bird provided he gave the bird his boots so that it didn't damage the onboard upholstery.

During the showing of 'The Ten Commandments' at Mount Hagen's cinema the audience stood, cheered and applauded when the Red Sea opened for the children of Israel to cross.

Sitting out in the middle of the Qattara Depression at night in the middle of a scouting trip, marvelling at the opportunity to view the wonders of a light-free sky.

A WWII landmine claimed the life of a young American technician when he drove over it in a Land Rover.

In a remote Iranian valley, looking like a photo from National Geographic, where the only facility the local people have is running water from a river, a young boy runs up to our jeep and yells 'David Beckham!' We smile and inwardly groan.

If we have to eat any more chicken kebabs out here I'm going to be sprouting feathers.

One of my most memorable Christmases was spent at a Save the Children official quarters in an old French fort in the small town of Messaad near Laghouat on the fringes of the Sahara in Algeria. Quite different from another old fort in the area overlooking unmarked graves of French legionnaires, the walls covered with names, dates, and bullet marks.

The level of xenophobia still evident; the result of the bitter war of independence.

Horrified at the sight of skinny boys slithering out of storm drains built into the kerbstones on the roads in Luanda, Angola. The city comes to a halt as the president's fifteen car convoy complete with ambulance and gun-toting escorts in wraparound sunglasses finally passes.

On Monday you make a mental note to help; by Friday the weekend beckons and all is forgotten. All you remember is the president made you late for lunch.

In 1966 after returning from active service in the 'undeclared war' which became known as 'Confrontation' in Sarawak, Borneo, my next adventure was the eastern region of Nigeria. It later became known as Biafra.

The company's motto was 'A life of science and adventure'.

Ananas

It was approaching dusk in Rue Duate Lopez. Two of Luanda's street urchins were sitting on the kerb of the broken sidewalk arguing over the sharing of a pineapple they had just stolen from a passing farm truck.

'Look Brito it was me that took the risk of grabbing it. All you did was make faces at the driver. It would have been me that would have been slashed, maybe killed even, if the guy riding shotgun hadn't been asleep.'

They had used their standard way of stealing from passing fruit and vegetable trucks at the corner of the street. One would pull faces at the driver as he slowed to negotiate the intersection while the other would scramble up the back of the truck and grab whatever they were carrying that day. It was also standard practice that the truck would have at least one labourer armed with a machete sitting in the back for such situations.

Only two months earlier Severino's best friend had died from a head wound received while operating this same routine. Severino had been lucky that time because he had been the decoy while his best friend Antonio had made the snatch. The guard had not been asleep that time. He was so unlucky. Normally they were too quick for whoever was sitting in the back but this day the guard had the drop on Antonio, and he paid with his life.

'You want to fight me for it?' Brito knew he was posing a rhetorical question. At twelve years old he was five years older than Severino and by far the bigger and stronger of the two. He was a pure-bred member of the Ovimbundu tribe and had the typical ebony black physique whereas Severino was a mixed-race mulatto; light brown and slight to the point of being skinny.

'You know I can't fight you. We're friends, aren't we? Antonio and me always shared. It never mattered who was doing the actual snatching. That's the way real friends co-operate. We don't need to argue or fight.'

'You talk too much.'

Before he could say another word, three much bigger youths appeared around the corner and seeing Brito with the pineapple, rushed at him with a high-pitched scream. They both shot to their feet, Brito tossing the swag to Severino, and leaping out into the road, he was gone in a flash.

Severino had but a split second to slip down the storm drain mounted on the side of the kerb, clasping the prized pineapple just before one of the three assailants had time to grab either him or the fruit. He didn't live in this particular drain but luckily it was the same size, and he was able to slip into it without grazing his body. Fortunately, the pineapple just slipped through as well. A larger piece of fruit and he would have been forced to leave it.

The three bigger boys were incandescent with rage. It was theirs for the taking, but this little bastard had outwitted them and there was no way any of them could fit into the drain.

'You'd better toss that pineapple out Severino, or this day might be your last.'

'It's mine. Go get your own dinner.'

'I said toss it out or we will smoke you out of there. You know how that goes don't you?'

Severino screwed up his eyes in an attempt to see if the drain offered him any chance of escape from the immediate vicinity but once his vision became adjusted to the darkness, he could see there was no way out. It was blocked a few feet either side of him. He knew these three and he knew they would take sadistic pleasure in stealing his fruit. If they smoked him out, he would not only lose his prized possession, but he would be choked and then most certainly beaten.

With a heavy heart he prepared to push the pineapple back through the drain but not before he spat on it and rubbed his spittle into the rough surface.

'Here, take it please and leave me in peace.'

'Well done, Severino, you really are learning the rules of the street. We'll let you go this time, you little cockroach.' One of them picked it up and they walked off down the street passing the pineapple basketball fashion between them as they went.

Severino waited until he couldn't hear them any more and climbed out of the drain. He was just about to head back to his home street when Brito reappeared from behind a rubbish trolley.

'Jeez that was close Sevee, I thought they might have got you. Did they get the pineapple?'

'Did they get the pineapple? Of course they bloody did and they nearly got me. Thanks for helping me friend. You were a great help, you were. I don't want to be your partner any more Brito. Go find someone else to work with. I'm going to find a job where I don't have to risk my life every day. See if you can find some other mug.' With that he scarpered off up the street before Brito could grab hold of him. He might not be able to fight him, but he could certainly outrun him in the narrow passages off the main street.

Father van der Bosch's Last Christmas

It was Friday, a week before Christmas, and Jens van der Bosch was walking through the alley from his residence in the walled city of Jerusalem. He had been invited for dinner by an old acquaintance, Maurice the manager of the Sinai Hotel, outside the old city walls.

Dusk was approaching, various craft and workshop vendors were either closing down their shutters for the night or busy rearranging their wares and checking the lighting. Though he knew most of them by sight and in some cases by name, he endeavoured not to offer any greetings in order to avoid the inevitable time-consuming cups of tea that would lead to his being late for his appointment.

As he silently walked through the labyrinth, turning this way and that, his feet knew the direction well, having trod this way so many times over the years; he was able to direct his thoughts into reflections rather than the need to concentrate on the route.

He had taken up this post as a novice at the age of 23; now he was nearing retirement in this year, on his 65th birthday. All too soon he would be a resident at the Franciscan retirement home in his native Holland. A slight chill came over him at the mere thought of it.

Where had the years gone? He smiled to himself as he remembered his first month, trying his utmost to blend in and learn the art of obsequiousness in order to fit in to the ways of this smouldering melting pot of the three major religions, without fear or favour.

Unexpectedly it had snowed the first week in January that year, something he never ever considered likely. He thought he had left snow and ice behind in Europe. But snow it did, and he fondly remembered the look of righteous indignation of the camel hunkered down outside one of the tourist hotels, a white blanket slowly forming on his head and hump. How silly and incongruous he looked.

So much had happened in the intervening years; some good, but mostly sad. That first year there had been much celebrating at the rescue of hostages in Entebbe. This was but the first of many significant events during his tenure and a classic example of the tenacity of this tiny nation to survive against overwhelming odds.

As he turned a sharp right out of the last alley that led to the main road to meet the hotel taxi, he almost collided with a young rabbi hurrying for the start of the Shabbat.

The rabbi nearly lost his hat and Jens offered his profuse apologies in English. Though he had mastered Hebrew as well as Arabic he still was not comfortable in the former.

'My sincere apologies Rabbi, I'm afraid I was lost in thought. May I offer you the season's greetings? Merry Christmas.'

The rabbi glared back, righted his black Homburg hat and attempted to continue on his way, but not before spitting loudly on the cobbles. Jens was extremely upset at such a response but in forty plus years he had learned a lot and not all from his calling or the bible. He had the advantage of middle age; the rabbi was but a young man and given to such outbursts.

He turned around, embracing the rabbi quietly but firmly and kissed him on each cheek. The rabbi recoiled and pushed him away - he had spent over an hour ceremoniously dressing and preparing for the lighting of the candles. Now this stupid priest had defiled him, and he would have to return to his home and begin the ritual all over again.

Father Jens van der Bosch continued on his way out onto the main street to the waiting taxi. Having greeted the driver with all the necessary politeness he settled into the back seat with a smile on his face. A life of many twists and turns, and the year was coming to its natural conclusion. But first he was to have supper with Maurice.

Ration Day at Cape Rodney

The moment Angus's eyes opened he realised it was Saturday and that meant only one thing for him – ration day for the workers on Bonguina, a coconut and cocoa plantation carved out of the tropical forests of coastal Papua. Today, like every Saturday, one labourer would test his physical capacity to manage them. To them it was no more than a game, whereas for Angus it was a matter of survival.

It was almost two years to the day since he took over the management of Bonguina Plantation. He wasn't sure what had possessed him to accept the job then, and every Saturday morning since. Initially it was fun; now it was about survival.

The truth was little planning or forethought had gone into Angus Duncan's life. Having migrated to Australia to join his older brother, he had difficulty in settling into a factory job in Sydney. There, the combination of a long commute between his home and the factory and the sheer mind-numbing boredom of factory work gave him little or no satisfaction.

Waves of homesickness threatened to overwhelm him. Australia offered huge open spaces, even more than his homeland, just as his brother had promised, but here he was, stuck in a huge metropolis with little or no time to experience the much talked about outback he had dreamed of.

It wasn't long before he started to have thoughts of returning home. Admitting defeat hung heavy on his mind. He endeavoured to counter such thoughts by spending every opportunity walking along various parts of the north shore. It was there he found a small café on a quiet beach with an attractive waitress called Kathy. A fellow Scot, she immediately caught his eye. As immigrants from the same part of the world it was only natural they quickly became good friends.

Their isolation and loss of family and friends back home created a magnetic attraction between them and romance soon blossomed.

They moved in together and married three months later. It eased the situation considerably, but before long he realised he simply couldn't stand the job or the city any longer. Opening his heart to a mate one lunch break, he discovered he had a friend who knew of a company that was looking for truck drivers in New Guinea. The pay was good and all he needed was a clean driver's licence.

Several letters and telegrams later he was interviewed at a breakfast table in a hotel in King's Cross, offered the job, and the couple flew up to Port Moresby and on to Mount Hagen. The company comprised of a group of hard-working, hard-drinking, British, Australian and Kiwi expatriates making big money risking life and limb, driving over perilous laterite roads in mountains that no mechanised vehicle had ever traversed before. Jokingly they nicknamed it the Highlands Highway.

Angus loved the job even if the road conditions scared him on a daily basis. But it meant Kathy was left back in Hagen in a wild frontier atmosphere. Her Celtic skin and blonde hair were too much of a temptation for the locals outside of their compound. They couldn't stay; she just couldn't stand it. They decided to return to Australia, maybe a smaller town this time when, out of the blue Angus was offered a position managing a plantation in Cape Rodney. They needed a replacement yesterday. The only qualifications required were that he was English speaking, numerate and spoke passable Pidgin.

Now two years later he was quietly turning these thoughts over in his mind. He was about to take part in the weekly life-threatening game of managing a bunch of men whose outlook and culture was not far removed from the Stone Age. Yet only last week they had listened enthralled to the ABC radio; America had successfully put a man called Neil Armstrong on the moon.

If only he had a trustworthy second in command, even a local assistant manager, he could delegate this weekly chore. Perhaps a local assistant would not create such a challenge and it could be settled amicably in dialogue. His requests fell on deaf ears; the company would not agree. He was told quite simply that his predecessor had managed several years on his own without complaint, and he wasn't even married.

He pulled the mosquito net aside and put his feet down onto the polished teak floorboards, grateful for the cool sensation under his feet. He tucked the net back into the mattress, glanced enviously at Kathy soundly sleeping, and tiptoed into the bathroom.

He showered quickly and quietly under the cold water, dried himself and pulled on the shirt and shorts he'd worn the day before. There was no sense in putting on clean clothes for Saturday morning until after the weekly roll call. He grabbed his tobacco tin and lighter from the bedside table and went downstairs.

It was just before seven and the labourers were beginning to appear in the yard that separated the manager's house from the office and warehouse. Beyond that were several buildings made out of corrugated zinc, containing the smoking kilns of copra. Behind these, in between the coconut palms, were two rows of dormitories constructed of locally hewn timber, handmade frond matting and roofed with corrugated zinc now discoloured by tropical rain, sunshine and the leaf droppings from the palms.

Angus rolled a cigarette, lit it and poked his head through the open upper half of the serving door of the storeroom. 'You got everything ready, Mario?' A brown face with a fuzzy stack of hair appeared around the corner of one of the shelves.

'Yes, Mister Angus, we'se ready sir.' Mario was a light-skinned coastal Papuan who was Angus's only English-speaking employee. He had been raised and educated in a Catholic orphanage in Port Moresby. Angus thought to himself, as he did every Saturday, Mario could be that assistant manager, if only he could control his light fingers. God knows he had told him often enough, but old habits are hard to break.

'Okay, get Chimbu to rouse them out then and let's get this over and done with. I only hope there aren't too many troublemakers this morning.' Chimbu was Mario's assistant. At forty years old he represented an influential elder to the rank and file of the labourers who were all in their late teens or early twenties. He came from the same tribe as the workers, a small region of the Sepik River valley.

Having grown up in the rarefied atmosphere of the highlands all these men had superb physiques and were the colour of mahogany.

By comparison, Angus looked a poor physical specimen with his thinning red hair and spindly frame that never took a tan. There was far too much Celtic blood in his veins for him to be anything but freckled and pale skinned, even though he never wore anything other than sleeveless shirts, football shorts and a battered old floppy hat and spent most days exposed to the cruel tropical sun.

The daily workforce had now assembled in six lines of ten all except one man, Niguan, who now came sauntering out adjusting his grubby work sarong.

'I might have known you'd be last,' Angus spoke matter-of-factly without either looking up or bothering to speak in Pidgin. A murmur went around the group. It was Saturday and Niguan was going to try his luck again.

Angus started to read off the names of the workers one by one adding the number of hours each one had worked that week. Everyone replied with a positive acknowledgement until it came to Niguan who came back with a sharp, 'No-got.' Angus carried on through the list as though he had not heard Niguan.

As he finished the list, he clipped the pencil onto the board and offered it to Chimbu who was standing directly behind him. He then looked directly at Niguan for the first time and beckoned him forward by a downward movement of his right hand.

No word was spoken but the parade suddenly dissolved from their six ranks and reformed into a rough circle, almost as a practised drill. In the centre stood Angus, expressionless. Facing him was Niguan, whose face had broken out into a huge grin, his forehead glistening with beads of perspiration, more from anxiety than the effects of the morning sun now starting to appear through the palm trees. They stood six feet apart and started to move in a crab-like clockwise direction. They looked like a couple of fighting cocks weighing each other up, daring the other to make the first move.

Suddenly, Niguan shot forward, arms outstretched in an attempt to grab Angus in a bear hug that would certainly crush him. But Angus had been here many times before and, as quick as his opponent was, he was far nimbler. His schoolboy boxing bouts served him well.

Angus sidestepped the rush, pulled down Niguan's outstretched right arm and head-butted him straight onto his now unprotected right cheekbone. The sound of Angus's forehead hitting Niguan's face was sickening. He went down with a loud smack as his sweating body hit the damp concreted yard. A cheer went up from the circle of men who jumped and clapped in appreciation.

Angus turned on his bare heel and said to Mario, who was watching from the serving hatch 'Fun and games over for another week. Give them their rations and make line. Better give Niguan a couple of aspirins. That cheek might ache a bit.'

Mario just smiled and nodded. Angus showed no outward sign of emotion, but his heart was beating almost loud enough to be audible. He had survived another Saturday.

He walked slowly back to the house. Once inside he started up the stairs but stopped on the second step. Kathy would still be asleep and there was no point in waking her. The anxiety of the job had affected his sexual desire considerably over the past year, so he reasoned there was little point in returning to bed at this time of the morning, and he certainly wouldn't be able to go back to sleep.

He turned back into the kitchen intending to make a pot of tea, but even this didn't appeal to him. Instead, he took a South Pacific Lager from the kerosene-fired fridge. He opened the bottle, took a swig from it and sat down at the table and started to roll another cigarette.

He puffed heavily on the cigarette, took another swig from the bottle and started to ponder his life and the impact these Saturday mornings had on him and Kathy.

Drifting back to his days as a young boy in Scotland, he remembered the times his father had chided him and his brother that they didn't know what fear and hardship was. He would regale them with stories of his service with the Argyll and Sutherland Highlanders in North Africa, and invariably ending up with saying, 'The Arabs were a bigger threat to my life than the Germans ever were. Aye, you two would have run home to yer mammie.'

'Aye da, with all your bloody stories inspired by Johnnie Walker, I wonder how you would have coped this morning with that big black bugger running at you? I didn't have a bayonet mounted on a 303 and mates to help me, da.' He found himself talking out loud, though his only companion was a gecko on the side of the fridge.

He felt sad, alone and depressed. Here he was, reduced to drinking beer and talking to himself at eight in the morning. Tears welled in his eyes.

Wiping away those tears he forced the thoughts from his mind, tossed the beer bottle into the waste bin and walked outside, hoping Mario had managed to finish the ration distribution without stashing a couple of extra tins for himself.

Mayday – the Mayaguez Incident

On a normal working day in Indonesia in early May 1975 I was sitting having an after-lunch coffee with the area manager from Singapore, and the Jakarta office manager of our company Delta Exploration, an American seismic company.

Our conversation was suddenly interrupted by the SSB radio in the adjoining radio room crackling into life with a Mayday call. The caller was male, clearly American and very much distressed. Having called 'Mayday' several times, the caller had now eventually been answered by the Filipino operator manning the small ships' radio watch in Manila.

The company did have ocean going vessels operating from time to time in the region but use of the radio channel was somewhat dubious in legal terms when used for transmissions from land-based operations.

Following procedure, the Filipino, radio operator's insistence on getting the vessel's name correct caused obvious distress to the American having to repeat the name.

John, who had written down Mayaguez correctly, picked up the microphone and said, 'Merchant vessel Mayaguez, do you copy?'

The reply put us in a bit of a quandary as the man then asked 'Who am I speaking to?'

'We are a private exploration company. What is your problem?'

'This is a United States merchant vessel. Our company is SeaLand, transiting the Gulf of Thailand, and we have been boarded by armed Cambodian military. They do not know I am transmitting this. Would you please inform the US authorities? I don't know how much longer I can transmit, and you might be the last person I ever speak to!' His voice was rising to the point of hysteria.

I went into another room and dialled the American embassy. I was lucky and got through the first time. The voice at the other end

158

said, 'This is the embassy of the United States of America. Who am I speaking to and what is the purpose of your call?'

I answered his question and he immediately responded by telling me to hold for a second. I heard several clicks and realized I was being connected to multiple phones. One of the connections asked me to repeat my story, name and street address.

'We will be there in ten. Keep them talking if you can,' and with that I was disconnected. I went back to the radio room to see what else was being said but we had lost contact. The ship's radio had obviously been discovered by the hijackers.

In just short of twenty minutes two white American Chevrolet Suburbans swung into the company driveway. I was impressed, knowing they made the journey in what I would describe as record time. I only wished local taxi drivers were as efficient in finding the address. Three tall, well-built young men strode into the office. The leader was dressed in a white naval uniform with officer's insignia on his epaulettes.

He asked first if we were still in contact and unfortunately, we had to say no. We tried several more attempts to call the ship but there was no reply. He then asked us to give him the outline of the conversation that had taken place and he listened carefully while one of the others took notes.

When we had finished the story as far as it went he relayed it via his hand-held radio. He thanked us for our help and as he was leaving I said to him, 'What do you think you will do?'

'If it was up to me I'd blast them out of the water. But, in reality, probably nothing.' With that they climbed back into their vehicles and left.

We in turn had another coffee and chatted about the part we had played in what had been quite an exciting change for a quiet afternoon in the Jakarta office. I have to say that I was rather in awe of John's ability to quickly and quietly respond to the emergency in such a laid back, matter-of-fact manner without any fuss or drama. It spoke volumes for the quiet Texan character that many an Englishman would mock more often than not.

A little while later a taxi arrived to take me to the airport. I couldn't wait to get to the crew and tell everyone what had happened back in Jakarta. I had my minute of fame and used it the max.

Being located in a relatively isolated place out in Sulawesi, we only received news from the real world via weekly letters and week-old newspapers, hand-carried by incoming personnel from Singapore. Imagine my surprise when I opened a copy of the Straits Times a week later and the bold headline read 'Mayaguez Incident – Ford sends in the marines,' or something to that effect.

It transpired that President Gerald Ford ordered his country's military forces to retake the Mayaguez and sent in the US Navy and Marine Corps. It went down in the history books as the last action of the Vietnam War. The thirteen marines who were killed during the rescue mission were the last military personnel to lose their lives in that war and it was the only time that the United States ever engaged Cambodia in military conflict.

Cape Rodney topographical survey by the author, Territory of
Papua and New Guinea, 1969

Printed in Great Britain
by Amazon